S0-AEN-592

THE SO BLUE MARBLE

DOROTHY B. HUGHES

Introduction by
OTTO PENZLER

Porter County Public Library

AMERICAN
MYSTERY
CLASSICS

Hebron Public Library
201 W. Sigler Street
Hebron, IN 46341

habfi   HEB
HUGHE

Hughes, Dorothy B. (Dorothy Belle),
The so blue marble
33410015045588   10/12/18

DISCARD

This is a work of fiction. Names, characters, places, and incidents either are the product of the author's imagination or are used fictitiously. Any resemblance to actual persons, living or dead, businesses, companies, events, or locales is entirely coincidental.

Published in 2018 by Penzler Publishers
58 Warren Street, New York, NY 10007
penzlerpublishers.com

Copyright © 1940 by Dorothy B. Hughes
Introduction copyright © 2018 by Otto Penzler
All rights reserved.

Cover image: Andy Ross
Cover design: Mauricio Diaz

Paperback ISBN 978-1-61316-105-0
Hardcover ISBN 978-1-61316-111-1

Library of Congress Control Number: 2018905469

Distributed by W. W. Norton

Printed in the United States of America

9 8 7 6 5 4 3 2 1

OTTO PENZLER PRESENTS
AMERICAN MYSTERY CLASSICS

THE SO BLUE MARBLE

DOROTHY B. HUGHES (1904–1993) was a mystery author and literary critic. Born in Kansas City, she studied at Columbia University and won an award from the Yale Series of Younger Poets for her first book, the poetry collection *Dark Certainty* (1931). After writing several unsuccessful manuscripts, she published *The So Blue Marble* in 1940, winning praise for its terse, hard-boiled prose.

Hughes published thirteen more novels, the best known of which are *The Fallen Sparrow* (1942), *Ride the Pink Horse* (1946), and *In a Lonely Place* (1947). All three were made into successful films. In the early fifties, Hughes largely stopped writing fiction, preferring to focus on criticism, for which she would go on to win an Edgar Award. In 1978, the Mystery Writers of America presented Hughes with the Grand Master Award for literary achievement.

OTTO PENZLER, the creator of American Mystery Classics, is also the founder of the Mysterious Press (1975), a literary crime imprint now associated with Grove/Atlantic; MysteriousPress.com (2011), an electronic-book publishing company; and New York City's Mysterious Bookshop (1979). He has won a Raven, the Ellery Queen Award, two Edgars (for the *Encyclopedia of Mystery and Detection*, 1977, and *The Lineup*, 2010), and lifetime achievement awards from Noircon and *The Strand Magazine*. He has edited more than 70 anthologies and written extensively about mystery fiction.

**Hebron Public Library
201 W. Sigler Street
Hebron, IN 46341**

THE SO BLUE
MARBLE

For my mother,
CALLA HALEY FLANAGAN,
who will not read mysteries,

and

For my brother,
FRANK SYLVESTER FLANAGAN,
who first introduced me to them.

INTRODUCTION

IN RECENT years, we have witnessed a renewed interest in the early women authors of hard-boiled and noir fiction. The entirety of Margaret Millar's writings has been re-issued, two of Patricia Highsmith's novels have been adapted for film, and the two-volume anthology, *Women Crime Writers*, released by Library of America, has brought back the works of some neglected female authors, leading to conversations about gender and the genre in the middle of the twentieth century. At the heart of all this interest is Mystery Writers of America Grand Master Dorothy B. Hughes.

With several of her most noted titles having come back into print, Dorothy B. Hughes has enjoyed a recent reappraisal by modern audiences. Megan Abbott, for example, identifies *In a Lonely Place* as the singular birthplace of American noir. Walter Mosley, in his introduction to a new edition of *The Expendable Man*, compares her prose to that of Raymond Chandler and James Ellroy and praises her writing for its "particular view of that road between our glittering versions of American life and the darker reality that waits at the end of the ride." Christine Smallwood's review in *The New Yorker* of that same novel, Hughes's last, celebrates the writer's fixation on difference, how it is created and defined.

While much of this praise has focused on those of Hughes's novels that exhibit a noir sensibility, identifying her as an early and influential voice in that style, such reviews miss the versatility displayed by the majority of the author's career, ignoring (willfully or not) some of her major successes. A writer who produced as many novels of espionage as she did suspense, who wrote extensively on Erle Stanley Gardner (including the definitive biography), and who dedicated a book to Eric Ambler, Hughes was not to be pigeonholed. Over the course of a forty-seven year-long career that began with poetry and ended with criticism, Hughes published fifteen crime novels—novels with spies, maniacal killers, rich characters, poor characters, rural Southwestern settings, urban Northeastern settings; her work has the variation typical of a mid-century writer working to keep up with rapidly-changing tastes. Unlike a typical author from the period, however, she wrote wonderful and original books even as she moved between modes.

Born Dorothy Belle Flanagan in Kansas City, Missouri, in 1904, she attended the University of Missouri, Columbia University, and the University of New Mexico. Early in her writing career she worked on newspapers and wrote poetry. *Dark Certainty* (1931), a book of poems, won an award in the Yale Series of Younger Poets competition. When she married Levi Allen Hughes, Jr., she settled in Santa Fe; they had three children. In 1939, she published *Pueblo on the Mesa: The First Fifty Years of the University of New Mexico*; she launched her career as a mystery writer the following year.

Published in 1940, Hughes's debut novel, *The So Blue Marble*, is a wild ride of a thriller in which a young woman is pursued by devilish forces. The book introduces Griselda Satterlee, a young actress who has left a career in Hollywood to pursue a life as a fashion designer in Manhattan. No stranger to New York high society, she takes up residence at her ex-husband's Madison Avenue apartment and happily settles into her new life in the city. She unexpectedly finds herself visited by two deadly twins accompanied by, of all people, her own estranged younger sister, who has learned new cruelties from her upbringing in Rome. The trio seeks a powerful blue jewel that they claim Satterlee's ex-husband possesses and they'll stop at nothing to obtain it—not even murder.

As you can tell from this brief description, the book's premise stretches credibility—and yet, from the first page, it pulls readers in, carrying them along with the same breathless momentum seen in Hughes's other works. Instead of alienating the audience, the fantastical storyline, set in a familiar, if rarefied, world, gives the novel an unsettling, uncanny tone. At any moment, the everyday life of these characters can collapse into madness—and it does.

Supernatural elements are rare in Hughes's other novels, but what really sets *The So Blue Marble* apart from her work as a whole is its Art Deco sensibility—visible in its stylish prose, its zig-zagging plot, the mystical roots of the marble and, of course, the tale's luxurious, delightfully modern upper-class setting. The fact that the book's nightmarish storyline unfolds in against this glamorous backdrop is likely what contemporary readers found so terrifying about the narrative. At the time of its publication, a review in *The New York Times* admonished, "if you wake up in the night screaming with terror, don't say we didn't warn you." Famed critic Will Cuppy described the novel as "impressive in wallop and so irresistible in manner," while Anthony Boucher wrote that it is "an unforgettable experience in sensation fiction."

After *The So Blue Marble*, Hughes went on to write many more mystery novels, several of which were made into successful films. An unfaithful but memorable adaptation of *In a Lonely Place* (1947), directed by Nicholas Ray, featured Humphrey Bogart and Gloria Graham, to whom Ray was married during the production. Bogart had bought the rights to the novel for his own production company because he loved the title and the premise but, by the time the story made it to the screen, virtually nothing was left of the book he loved.

The adaptation of *The Fallen Sparrow* (1942), filmed one year later and starring John Garfield and Maureen O'Hara, was much more faithful to Hughes's novel about a former prisoner in the Spanish Civil War who comes to New York to find the man who murdered the NYPD lieutenant who had helped him escape. The film changed the torture venue to a Nazi POW camp but otherwise adhered to the storyline.

Ride the Pink Horse (1946) was also quickly filmed and released only a year after Hughes's novel was published; it was directed by and starred Robert Montgomery and is today considered a noir classic. The book is a taut thriller about a mysterious tough guy who comes to a New Mexico border town at the time of its annual Mexican Fiesta searching for a man in order to kill or blackmail him; it is also a significant cultural landmark that provides a rare look at the three cultures that had fused in New Mexico, describing the collision of Mexican, Native American, and Anglo societies.

Although *The So Blue Marble* was Hughes's debut novel, it feels remarkably mature and fully realized. The book may be less well-known than some of her later titles because of the outstanding films they inspired, but it is the equal of her other works, even being selected by Howard Haycraft and Ellery Queen as one of the cornerstone works in the history of mystery fiction. It is essential reading not only for those interested in this distinguished author, but for any that enjoy a great, unpredictable, classic mystery.

—OTTO PENZLER

I

HER DRESS was black and her coat, with its black fox collar, but at night no one would know the fox was real. Her hat didn't look as if it were a creation. Not at night, not with her pale horn-rimmed glasses; no one would look twice at a girl with glasses over her face.

Fifth Avenue was lighted, not with neon as Broadway, but it wasn't dark. Off the crosstown bus at Fiftieth, past the Cathedral, dark, yes, but there were people walking towards her and away from her, a young couple, students returning from a Carnegie concert, a goodly dressed man with heavy English brogans striding past her. And the windows beyond were light, the cosmetician's with the white down pussy cats pretending to grow on real pussy willow branches, the window of hand-created silver, the silver-etched imported china—bright candles on a bright street.

Only five blocks to Fifty-fifth, only a half block down with a great hotel on the corner and chipmunk taxi drivers waiting for the carriage trade. Her key ring was tight in her black gloved hand, her black antelope purse tight under her arm.

No reason to feel nervous at night, not even at eleven-thirty at night, in the heart of New York. Nothing ever happened to her kind of people; things happened to people living down those cross streets in old red bricks or old brownstones. Things threatened silver and gold dancers there in the Iridium Room across. But things didn't happen to her or anyone she knew.

Five short blocks and the sound of her black heels striking the walks. There were other sounds but she didn't hear anything but the heels. The other walkers didn't seem to notice that hers were too loud. She crossed Fifty-fifth, turned down her side of the street.

One delighted voice said, "Griselda! Fancy seeing you!"

The other one was laughing. "We thought you'd never come!"

She could see the tall silk hats, the shining white scarves, the dark coats, the sticks under their arms. Even in shadow she knew she had never seen the faces.

She was pleasant although wary. "I'm afraid you've made a mistake." Princeton boys or Yale, with a bit too much. But one had called her by name, by her own name.

One of them laughed. "Why, Griselda, how you talk!"

The other said, "And you so late for your appointment!"

"And we so patient."

They were moving her down the street as soldiers moved a condemned man. There wasn't a policeman. There never was at night in this neighborhood, by day yes, riding his fine horse, keeping traffic moving, but not at night. And Con was thousands of miles away.

She spoke insistently, "There's some mistake. You know there is. You've never seen me before."

They laughed uproariously. They had nice laughs, college boy laughs. She almost laughed with them, they were so merry. But each had a hand, ever so softly, under her elbow and she couldn't stop walking. They were moving her, even while they laughed, down the street to the two half-lighted windows, in one a swath of printed silk, in one two antique vases and an ostrich plume. If you turned between the shop windows, you went down a slightest incline to the door. It was locked at six. You opened it with your latch key, stepped into a small parquet vestibule; you rang for the elevator and waited. It was a self-running elevator, like in hospitals and old French pensions. Maybe that was why she was nervous, hearing her heels noisy on Fifth Avenue at night. She didn't like the feel of being shut in that elevator. But nothing happened to her kind. You pushed the four button and the car stopped at four. And then you were safe in Con's apartment, looking out of the windows, down at the cabs below, looking across the street where tall silk hats and furs came out of a great hotel.

She could say to these two, "Listen to me! A joke is a joke, boys, but you know that you don't know me and I don't know you and I want to go home now. If you don't stop this nonsense I'll speak to one of the drivers."

Suppose they didn't stop it? She could even speak to the taxi drivers. And suppose they just laughed too, or ignored her, thought she was crazy? She knew what she would do, walk past that entry way, pretend she lived farther on. Cross Madison, on the corner another hotel and a brightly lighted cocktail bar. She'd go in there and speak to someone. She didn't want to speak to the taxi drivers.

They were at the entrance to Con's. She moved her feet straight ahead, kept her eyes straight ahead, but two gloved hands gently on her two elbows veered her to the door.

She said, "You're making a mistake. I don't live here."

They laughed softly and the one on her left said, "You wouldn't fool us, would you, Griselda?" while the other opened her hand and took away her keys. He had the door open and held it for her. She didn't know what to do. She could run. She could scream. But she couldn't do either. She was afraid. It was a dream and whatever she did there would be one on either side of her making her turn their way. But this couldn't be real. She'd never seen either of them before.

If she could reach the bells and push Gig's. He might be at home although he wasn't usually in this early. But one stood between her and the bells.

She was almost tearful with helpless rage. "I don't know why you're acting this way. You don't know me. You know you don't."

Hands walked her inside. Others closed the door. They were on either side of her again and one rang for the elevator. She could hear it creaking its way down the shaft.

One said to the other, "I don't think Griselda likes us."

The other put out his lower lip. "I don't know why. We like us."

They had such nice faces, as much as she could see of them, with the hats tilted over their eyes, the scarves high to their chins.

One held the elevator door. The other said, "You first, Griselda," but his hand was still soft on her arm white she stepped in. They followed, closed the door. One pushed button four.

She was cold now. "I don't know what this is all about. I don't know how you found out my name or where I'm staying. But I do think you're carrying a joke too far."

She had a fleeting suspicion that perhaps this was Con's idea of sport, or Gig's. But not Gig. He was too serious. Whatever it was she didn't like it. The elevator stopped. One was out; one behind her. One opened the door of her apartment, Con's apartment. They were inside, the door closed, the lights on. She stood in the middle of the floor watching them remove their tall hats, their white kid gloves, their white silk scarves, black formal overcoats; watching them lay down their sticks with the old-fashioned gold knobs topping them; watching them until they stood there, between her and the door, fashion plates in tails, white ties, opera pumps.

And only then was she really afraid, and for such a fantastic reason. Because one had honey-colored hair, sleek to his head, and one had bat-black hair; one had very blue eyes and one very black; one had the golden tan coloring of blonds and one the olive tan coloring of brunettes. But outside of that they looked exactly alike, unbelievably, frighteningly, alike. It was as if an artist had taken the same photograph and colored one dark, one fair. They were identical twins. And she was afraid.

The dark one was lighting a cigarette. The light one pulled up a comfortable cushioned chair. It was between her and the door. The dark one said, "Con won't mind if we have a drink. Will you join us, Griselda?"

She didn't answer but her fear ebbed. They did know Con. And they knew the apartment because the dark one opened the door into the tiny cupboard kitchen and she could hear bottles and glasses. She took off her coat then, standing there in the middle of the floor, and her glasses. They were such handsome men and she'd forgotten about wearing glasses. She put these on the mantel. The blond one took her coat and he opened the enormous closet of the living room, hung it on a hanger. She couldn't get to the entrance without passing him and even if she did it took two hands to turn that special bolt and open the door. She wasn't frightened now anyway. It was one of Con's jokes, something he considered funny.

The twin in the kitchen called out, "Bourbon or Scotch, Danny?" and the blond one came away from the closet.

"Bourbon, if it's good. Otherwise no. And what will you have, Griselda?"

She put her bag and gloves and hat on the table and sat on the couch. Danny sat beside her. She said, "I'll have a glass of sherry." He passed her a cigarette from the box on the table but for himself took one from a case out of his pocket. His cigarette was a French one with a small gold D engraved on the tip. The letter really was engraved. She knew without feeling it.

He called back, "Griselda will join us with a glass of sherry, David."

He was the best-looking man she'd ever seen until David came in with the drinks and then he was. They both were. David sat in the easy chair that Danny had placed. Danny remained beside her on the couch. But she wasn't afraid now. She sipped the sherry.

She spoke lightly, "Won't you tell me now what this is all about?"

David drank. "Not bad Scotch. How's the Bourbon, Danny?"

"Not bad at all."

"Did Con plan this? And why? Tell me about it." She was eager now to know. "I was frightened at first when you spoke to me and came in here. Who are you?"

They laughed again, those joyous laughs of theirs, and she laughed too, and then she stopped with something like a shiver. She didn't know why. Maybe because David was looking into his glass and his face wasn't laughing. Only his throat was. Maybe because she couldn't see into Danny's blue eyes. They were like jewels, not real.

He said, "Still pretending you don't know us, Griselda?"

She put her wineglass down and she sat very straight and stiff. "I don't know you." It seemed as if she'd been saying those words for hours. "I've never seen you before. I don't know who you are. You don't know me." She was a little hysterical. "Are you friends of Con's? You must be. Are you? What are you doing here?"

David pretended to sigh. "You aren't very hospitable, Griselda."

She was near to tears again but she buffeted them. "If you don't tell me right away what this is all about, I'll call the police."

Danny said, not too quickly, but easily, "I don't think you'd do that, Griselda."

David spread his thin hands, steel hands, you could tell. "What would you tell the police? Two young men escort you home, enter your apartment with you, the door opened by your own key, join you in a quiet drink. You couldn't say we were housebreakers nor disturbers of the peace. You could say we attacked you, I presume, but you'd have to tear yourself up a bit first. We wouldn't lay hands on you. And even then—"

She knew she was beaten. They wouldn't permit her to call the police anyway. She said, "You win. I'll be good. What do you want?"

David said, "We've just come to get our marbles."

Danny said, "That's all. Then we'll finish our drinks and leave you."

Then David looked at her and she was frightened again. His eyes, too, were jewels, not real, oblong black stones. You couldn't see into them nor beneath them. He smiled. "We want our marbles. In particular one marble, a very blue one."

Danny was pleasant "We don't care about the others. Just give us our very blue marble and we'll go."

She held to her nerves. Maybe it was a dream, or maybe she was shut up in a crazy place. She wouldn't let go, scream and laugh and cry the way she wanted to. She tried to be natural, to be matter-of-fact. She couldn't help laughing a little.

"I haven't your marbles. There aren't any marbles here. You can look."

They didn't say anything.

She said, "I'll buy you some tomorrow when the stores open. I'll send you some if you wish me too. I'm sorry I haven't any for you now."

The dark David had stood up and he walked over to her until he was right in front of her. She was so frightened, for no reason, that she was shaking. He said, "We only want one marble, Griselda. The very blue one."

She screamed then. She didn't know why. Something about his eyes that were so dark, so opaque. Three things happened at once. She screamed. Danny's thumb and forefinger caught her wrist not softly now, but as if they were pincers. And someone pounded on her door. Three more things happened. She stopped her scream, Danny's fingers were on her knee, and there was a call, "Griselda, are you home?"

David spoke softly, "You answer it Griselda."

She was afraid to walk to that door, her back to the twins, but she did. She didn't hurry but she wanted to.

And outside was Gig, not six feet tall, not black handsome, nor golden handsome, not in evening attire. Just Gig, hardly taller than she, nondescript hair not combed very well, round spectacles over his round gray eyes, his old tweed working jacket over his pajamas, a book in his hand. She almost flung her arms around him. Gig, nice, sane Gig.

He said, "I didn't know you had company. I heard you come in and I'd just found that passage—"

She spoke rapidly, shrilly, on top of his words. "Come in. I'm not at all busy." She clung to his arm, pulled him inside. When she turned, the twins had their sticks under their arms, their hats on their heads.

Danny said, "We're just leaving."

David said, "It's been fun seeing you, Griselda."

They had their coats, their scarves, their gloves as they spoke.

She sidled Gig and herself past the door, leaving it wide for them.

Danny echoed, "Great fun, Griselda. See you soon."

"See you soon," David agreed.

They closed the door behind them. She heard them open the heavy elevator door; it was waiting, no one had used it since they had come up. She heard the whine of the machinery taking the cage downward. Only then did she release Gig's arm. She plopped down on the floor and began to laugh and cry, to cry and laugh.

2

Gig said, "Stop it! Stop it, Griselda!" He looked so utterly bewildered, woebegone, she laughed harder, cried harder. But she choked out, "Bolt that door. Lock and bolt that door."

He told her, "It is bolted. It bolts itself, Griselda. Are you crazy?"

She hugged her knees. "I think I am. Somebody's crazy. Or everybody's crazy." She couldn't stop the awful noises she was making.

He said, "You've got to stop it. You'll make yourself sick." Then he had an idea. He went into the kitchen and poured out half a tumbler of Scotch. He knelt down and pushed it op to her mouth. She drank it. It made her choke but it quieted her.

He helped her up from the floor to the couch. "Now can you tell me? What's happened?"

She said she didn't know. She began, "Does Con play mar— mar—mar—" Then she started laughing again but she stopped herself. She couldn't say it without laughing. It was too ridiculous. Leggy Con, on the floor shooting marbles.

Gig was troubled. He begged, "Try and tell me, Griselda." He was so sane. "Or don't if you'd rather not."

She caught his hand. "I want to tell you. Let me have a cigarette first. Then maybe I can make sense."

He found the box, as usual he had only a smelly pipe in his pockets, and lit her cigarette.

She leaned against the pillows. "I'll tell you. I've been nervous ever since I came, Gig, all this past week. I don't know why. Every night I've been sort of—well,—frightened—coming home from the theater, or from Ann's. Whenever I've been out alone, I've been—well, just plain scared."

She didn't expect him to understand. He didn't. He blinked behind his spectacles. He wasn't an imaginator.

She explained, "Not really scared, Gig. Just uneasy." She twisted on the couch until she could see his face. "Do you suppose something inside of us has premonitions—warns us to be careful? And yet if anyone had definitely told me, I'd have laughed. I'd have told them what I told myself. Things don't happen to people like us."

He was packing his pipe. "Well, they don't happen to people like me. But I'd say from what Con has told me that quite a lot has happened to you in your twenty-four years."

"Oh, that. I don't mean that." She was impatient. "I mean things like—horrible things—" She shivered a little.

He was startled. "Was tonight horrible?"

She could tell it now, although it didn't sound horrible, nor even as insane as it had been in happening. She told of the corner meeting, the entrance, all but the marbles. She couldn't speak of that yet.

He asked, puzzled. "They called you by name? And you didn't know them?"

"I've never seen them before in all my life. It might have been a joke. Do you think—did Con know them? Have you seen them before?"

He hadn't. "Of course I don't know about Con. He has multitudes of friends. I don't know many of them by sight or otherwise. Living across the hall as we do we still don't see much of each other. You know New York. That's why I was surprised to see you. I didn't even know you were coming East."

She said, "I know," but she wasn't thinking about Gig's surprised face when he came out of his apartment and saw her, surrounded by bags, opening the door of Con's apartment. She was thinking of marbles, of the ludicrousness of Con and marbles.

He asked, "You don't know who these men are?"

It wasn't a question but she answered, "They called each other David and Danny." She repeated, "David—Danny."

He was thoughtful. "There's Dave Cling—used to be on the *Times* with Con, but it wasn't he." And then he asked, all at sea, "But what did they want?"

She could tell him now, speak the insane words soberly, "They wanted their marbles."

Gig's mild eyes blinked.

"Particularly a very blue marble." She let him take it in before asking, "Does that mean anything to you?"

He repeated, "Their marbles—a very blue marble."

She asked, "Did Con ever play marbles?"

"My God, no!" He said, "I've never heard anything like it. Marbles—blue marbles—"

"One blue marble," she corrected.

He was thoughtful, "Do you think they were crazy?"

She nodded. "Part of the time I thought so, but"—she had to admit it—"they were saner than I was."

"Were they—" he didn't know how to phrase it—"did they offer any violence to you?"

She said they didn't, then she remembered tight fingers on her wrist, but she didn't correct herself.

He wondered, sucking at his pipe, if they should notify the police. She shook her head. "There's nothing to notify about that I can see. They didn't do anything. Besides I don't know who they are." She yawned. That tumbler was beginning to have effect.

He asked, "I don't suppose you've seen anything of any marbles around here—or one blue marble?"

She yawned again. "Of course not, Gig. I haven't gone through Con's boxes in there, nor the drawers he left filled. But I don't think I'd find marbles if I did."

"I don't imagine that you would," he agreed. "It is strange. It's

the strangest thing I've ever heard of. What can we do? What can
I do?"

She stood on her feet, a little dizzy from the dose. She said,
"You can stay here tonight."

"I couldn't do that!"

She was firm. "You'll have to. Or let me stay with you. I won't
be alone, Gig. I'm afraid."

He twittered, "I couldn't stay all night with you, Griselda."

"You must. I wouldn't dare be alone."

He didn't believe the men would return, but he didn't speak
with much sincerity.

She told him, "You heard what they said."

He had heard. But he didn't think they'd return tonight.

She was serious, yawning again. "It would be like them to come
back tonight. They are—" She couldn't find the word.

He supplied, "Erratic."

"Yes. Crazy." She started to the bedroom but her toes stopped
on the edge of the rug. "You don't mind looking in there first, Gig?"

He stammered, "N-no. Of course I don't." He was a professor
and not very tall but his shoulders were brawny.

Only two rooms at Con's, an old apartment building in the
middle of the city. Shops on the street floor and the first floor.
Only four floors of apartments, two to the floor, and the small single above where the superintendent lived. Fourth floor was safe,
Con's on the front, Gig's on the back. Two rooms at Con's, the great
high-ceilinged living room with the wood-burning fireplace, the
extra large closet, the cupboard kitchen; bedroom with the same
high ceiling, the like fireplace, a smaller closet, and a great bathroom. No way to get into the bathroom but the bedroom door and
a small skylight window opening into a shaft. But in the bedroom
a door leading to the backstairs which you must use if the elevator was out of order or stuck. Con had warned of the peculiarities

of the elevator but it hadn't gone wrong in her week of residence. Double bolts on the door to the backstairs. Each night she had peered at those bolts, making certain they were caught. But she hadn't touched them; she was afraid something might be standing outside. She heard Gig there now opening those bolts and the door. She shivered. She heard him close and bolt again.

When he returned he said, "It's perfectly safe. I even looked in the shower curtain and under the bed." No one could get under that low-set modern bed. He felt the stem of his pipe. "But if you're afraid I will stay here on the couch."

She said, "No, you won't. You'll stay in the bedroom. I'll sleep in a chair and you take the bed. Or if you insist I'll help you move the couch in there. But I won't stay alone." She touched his sleeve. "I'm not afraid of you, Gig. I'm afraid of them."

He didn't look at her. "Whatever you say, Griselda." He began picking up the empty glasses and taking them to the kitchen. She went in the bedroom but she didn't close the door between. For his sake she undressed in the bathroom, put on her white satin pajamas and her white tweed man-like dressing gown. She turned down the bed and called to him.

He came in. He said, "I suppose I shouldn't have washed the tumblers."

She shook her head. "Of course not. Bette comes at nine."

"I mean fingerprints."

Her mouth made an O. "I didn't think. But it wouldn't do any good." She took two extra blankets from the old cherrywood cabinet. "There's no reason for either of us to sleep in the chair. The bed's enormous. I'll sleep inside and you out." She felt mid-Victorian, but he was such a mouse. She spoke coaxingly, "You'll be more comfortable than in a chair and you have to teach tomorrow."

He was like a little boy. "All right, Griselda." He took off his spectacles and laid them on the left bed table.

She put her white coat on the foot of the bed and edged into the right-hand place. He lay far at the left and pulled the blankets over him. He didn't remove his coat.

She asked, "Do you think it would hurt to leave one lamp on?"

He didn't complain but he did say, "I can't sleep with a light on."

He had been too helpful. She turned out the lamp. It was like being in bed alone, but she could hear breathing. She felt safe. Then she asked, "What did you mean—plenty of things happen to me?"

He was apologetic. "It seems as if they do. Going to California four years ago to visit your aunt, like any popular society girl, and having the movies insist on starring you. Being really a great star when barely out of your teens—then leaving pictures entirely in one year despite all the offers they made. And now starting out again as a designer—" He broke off, "Con told me this."

She yawned. "Uh-huh. But that isn't really having things happen. I just photograph."

He said professorially, "Acting takes more than photography. Although you have beauty."

She didn't answer. People thought she had beauty. She didn't. Regular features were to be expected in ordinary people, and gray eyes were nothing. Hers looked big and bright because she needed glasses. Without glasses the straining widened the pupils. Her only real beauty was her hair, freak hair, naturally golden. It had retained unaided the gold of a child's hair, of a princess. She liked the way she wore it now, like a wig it was, turned below her ears, smoothed away from her forehead. Her skin and figure were good but that too was ordinary, to be expected when one swam and danced and rode and didn't gorge on sugars. Nothing sensational about her. She had hated being in the pictures even that one year, being fussed over.

He wondered, "Perhaps they had seen you in pictures."

She said sleepily, "But they called me by my own name, Grisel-da—not Mariel York. And I've been off the screen three years."

He spoke as sleepily, "That's right."

She was almost sliding into deep sleep when he spoke again.

"I really don't like staying here. Con is my friend."

She broke in rudely, "Don't be ridiculous. You know Con and I have been divorced for four years."

II

SHE OPENED her eyes wide and startled. She must have expected to see those twin faces but the room was empty and there was sun chinking through the Venetian blinds. The extra blankets were folded neatly on the chair. The sound in the other room was the maid. Bette alone picked her feet up and laid them down with such softness and placidity.

Then the phone rang again and she jumped a little. It was that which had wakened her, of course. She reached into the lower shelf of the bed stand and took it off the cradle.

Ann's voice answered her salutation. "Griselda—I've been calling and calling. Don't you ever get up? It's almost eleven."

Her sister always sounded a little distressed, just as if she weren't surrounded by servants and all care-lifting attentions.

Griselda said, "That's not so late. What inspired you to be up at this hour?"

Ann was humorless. "You know I take my lemon juice and coffee at nine-twenty every morning, Griselda, and see the children before they go to the park. And there's the menu to be gone over and the thousand things to do when you keep house—"

Griselda found a cigarette and held the phone by her shoulder while she lit it. She interrupted then, "I know." She asked lazily, "Anyway, what's so important about waking me before eleven?"

Ann spoke brittlely, "I have a wireless from Missy."

Griselda leaped up from her elbow. "You have what?" she shouted and heard Bette's work stop surprised.

Ann said, "You needn't yell. She is arriving today. Her boat docks at three."

Griselda spoke quickly, "I can't take her in with me. There isn't room. Besides these are bachelor apartments and I'm just borrowing Con's and he—"

This time her sister interrupted. "I'm not asking you to take her, Griselda, but you know I haven't an inch of room here. If I had I'd have asked you to stay with us although you didn't suggest it or even let me know you were planning a trip to New York. But I'd want you here if I had room—"

Griselda inserted, "I know it, darling—but Missy—what on earth inspired Maman to send her here, do you imagine?"

"I don't know. Maybe she just came. Didn't ask—"

They would meet for lunch at one at Maillard's, decide then what to do about the youngest. Griselda replaced the phone and put out her cigarette. Missy had always been a problem, a brat, to speak frankly, even if she was their own sister. She'd been solved by living abroad with their mother, likewise a brat, and the Italian prince stepfather. For how long? Six or seven years; Missy must be about sixteen now, eight years younger than Griselda, ten younger than Ann. Coming to New York, alone, evidently—they hoped alone. And what to do with her? Ann wouldn't take her, not Ann upset her well-ordered existence. And Griselda couldn't.

"And I won't," she said cheerfully, aloud.

Maybe Missy would like to go to camp in Maine, or there was always poor, dear, long-suffering Aunt Charlotte in Pasadena, Father's sister, and her equally long-suffering husband.

Griselda wrapped herself in her tweed and went into the living room. Bette was polishing at windows. She said, "Good morning," in her slight accented voice and her shy smile. "I bring the papers in, Miss Satterlee."

"Thank you, Bette." She opened the refrigerator, took out the glass of orange juice, iced now, which the maid had fixed. She didn't close the box then. She stood with one hand holding it. On top were three ash trays, set out by Bette to be cleaned. And in two were white stubs with small gold D's engraved on them. Last night was real again. She let the box door swing from her hand. She took the percolator from the tiny gas range, poured black coffee, carried it and the juice to the bedroom. She returned for the papers, *Times, Tribune, Mirror* and *News,* and her amber-rimmed glasses on the mantel. An orgy of papers was part of New York. She climbed into bed again, her breakfast on the table beside her. Plenty of time, Maillard's was only a few blocks down Madison, and Ann's one meant one-thirty.

Last night couldn't have been real. Yet in the ash tray... If she could only write Con. But she didn't know where, and if she did know, he might think she was trying to make up to him. She lit a match noisily, her cheeks reddened. She would not write Con even if she knew where. It was good of him to offer the apartment. Yes. But what had he said? Impersonal as a cricket. She knew it by heart.

"Sweet," he had started. That was sarcasm, or it meant nothing. He called all girls by endearments.

"Read in the papers that the great Hollywood designer known in private life as Griselda Cameron Satterlee (that Satterlee's a nice touch) is planning a two months' visit to her former home in New York, the first in four years. You're welcome to my apartment if you want it. I'll be on the border for that long, commenting on the situation there. I'll leave the keys with the superintendent. Get them if you want.

"Con."

And the postscripts:

"1. Sometimes the elevator sticks. Use the back door in that case.

"2. You'll have to take Bette with the apartment. She's a nice gal; chars for me and Gig. Six dollars per week.

"3. Gig bunks across the hall. You know, J. (for Joseph) Antwerp Gigland, professor of Persian Art at Columbia. Maybe you don't know. He's since your time. But if you want anything, holler."

That was all. It was nice to have the apartment, privacy, comfort, convenience—she hated hotels. And she wouldn't try to get in touch with him. Not if he had an apartment full of blue marbles and strange twins running in and out at all hours.

She sipped the strong coffee, read Winchell, Hellinger, Skolsky. She turned the pages idly and *their* picture stared into her face, one dark, one light. The headline said, "The Montefierrow twins at El Morocco last night." The outlines said, "Danver Montefierrow (l)," that was the light one, "and his twin brother, Davidant Montefierrow (r)," with his black hair and eyes, "at gay El Morocco last night."

She read the gossipy social column. "The Montefierrow brothers returned to Manhattan yesterday after twelve years' residence on the continent." There was nonsense about the loss to London night life and Paris and Rome, and of course the Riviera. She didn't pay much attention to it. They were real. And they weren't sinister. They were sons of the late William Danver Montefierrow, onetime senator, one-time governor, one-time head of the Madison National Bank, of the Pennsylvania Railroad, and two stickfuls more. They were also sons of the late Marie Davidant Montefierrow whose tragic death in Paris three years ago from an overdose of sleeping tablets, and so forth and so on.

Marie Davidant had been a friend of her mother's. And much

like her mother, too—fluttery, too often married. The twins were normal. Last night was a joke, something of Con's, or her mother's idea of an introduction.

She dressed now, in her red rust tweeds, the coat lined in beaver. March was always bitter in New York and today's sun after yesterday's rain meant additional chill. Not like California. She wouldn't be frightened any more, not of any Montefierrows. She wouldn't bother Gig again.

She left the door open while she rang for the creeping elevator. There was a moment when she was encased in it. But she wasn't frightened now. Nothing to be afraid of.

2

Ann was late. Griselda sat in a high-backed chair in the safety of the restaurant, there in front on the Madison side. Maillard's always smelled of chocolate and looked of dignified dowagers and correct children. She smoked her cigarette and was hungry.

Ann was so perfect, in black as was always most of smart New York, her gloves white as April orchards. Ann always wore white gloves. She had height and the right face.

She said, "I'm sorry to be late, Griselda," as they went up the few steps into the vast room of tables. Everyone looked at Ann, not openly but wishfully. She was perfection. There was art in the removing of her gloves, lifting the menu. There was art in everything Ann did with her hands. It was too bad she was irritating.

"Is the brook trout nice, Paul? And a mixed green salad and tea. And some of your lemon ice later, mixed with pineapple sherbet."

Griselda ordered tomato soup, lobster salad and coffee and felt like a clod. She repeated what she had thought out.

"I cannot take Missy in, Ann. After all it is mere accident that I'm here. In California—yes, I'd see to her. But this is your home. You are head of the family here." You had to be final with Ann. Even then you weren't sure of getting your own way.

Ann said, "If I had room..."

No use telling her to move the children into one nursery, or turn Arthur's dressing room into a temporary guest room. Ann did not disturb her setting.

Griselda was determined for once. She suggested, not as solution, but because the soup vapor was good to smell. "We might wait until she gets here. Maybe she has ideas of her own. After all she's sixteen." She did not add, "I was hardly older when I married." Her past marriage wasn't a favorite subject with Ann. Ann had done it right: St Thomas', with pews of money and family.

Ann agreed. "Maybe she's improved."

They both remembered that fat too curly face, all white fur and muff, leaning against the deck rail. Nasty little Missy.

Ann touched napkin to lips and tasted her dessert. She said, "I can't go with you to the boat, Griselda."

She had known Ann would get her own way. She spoke hotly, "That isn't fair!" and bitterly, "but you've never been fair."

Her sister's fingers poised. "Fairness has nothing to do with it, Griselda. This is Allen's day for his teeth and I have to take him. Cornelia has a slight cold and Nana has to stay with her."

Griselda repeated between set lips, "It isn't fair. But I'll bring her right to your apartment."

"Do. I've planned dinner for you, too. We can discuss plans with Missy then. Arthur will be there."

And he's as bad as you are, Griselda didn't say out loud. Only worse, for he goes your way.

Ann put bills on the silver plate. Griselda didn't protest. Let Ann pay for the lunch. She hated Ann. She had always hated her.

"It's almost three." Ann's wrist watch was smaller than a breath but more heavily diamonded. "You'd better take a cab."

Griselda said, "Yes." You couldn't say to Ann, "I've no intention of walking to the pier." You could say it but it wouldn't do any good.

She repeated brutally, "As soon as I get Missy, we'll come." She wouldn't let Ann shirk this. She had enough on her mind, marbles, Con, without a teen problem child.

She hailed a cab. It crawled through crosstown traffic until it was past Broadway. Then it lurched. The *Queen Mary* was in dock. She took the elevator up to the pier. There were passengers and passengers and too much luggage. The customs men were braided between.

She didn't know Missy. She hadn't thought of that before. Missy didn't know her. Missy didn't even know she was in New York.

The two of them came galloping along the wooden pier. They were late, obviously late. They didn't see her. She saw them first and she shrank into luggage and customs' uniforms. They weren't in tall hats now; their hats were brown, back on their heads; their suits were browny tan, Scotch woven, and their boots English brown. Their brown overcoats fled behind them. Their sticks were under their arms.

They didn't see her but she watched them until they came to a lovely girl. Blond Danny caught the girl up in his arms and kissed her five or six times, on cheeks and nose, chin and mouth, and the girl laughing with delight. Then dark David pushed Danny aside and held the girl too tightly and her tiny hands tight against his shoulders.

She hadn't noticed this one before; she'd been looking for school girls. This was exquisite, tiny, not as high by far as the twins' shoulders. Her hair was the color of the lemon ice Ann had spooned at lunch, maybe a shade darker, but not much. It was cut off square as a Dutch doll's, banged over dark arrow brows, square against pink cheeks. She wore a dark skullcap, like a Cardinal, on the back of her head. It was so far back, she looked hatless. Her mink coat was the darkest, the finest, Griselda had ever seen, even in movie star land. It was long and shawled, and beneath it you could see the exquisite frock, black with a touch of lemon ice at the throat.

The twins spoke to her a moment, turned, and Griselda shrank again. They left the pier as quickly as they had come. Then she walked in the girl's direction. It wasn't true. It couldn't be true. But it was Ann's nose and pointed chin, and the lemon hair tossed as Maman's used to toss.

The girl cried out joyfully, "Griselda!" She asked, not believing, "Are you Missy?"

"But of course I'm Missy!" She flung her arms about her sister and kissed her on both cheeks. "And you're Griselda."

Griselda was curious and she felt something strange within her, something cold. She asked, "How did you know me? I wouldn't know you."

Missy had a tinkling laugh. "But of course. I have changed from child to woman. You are the same." There was something foreign in her shoulders, her phrasing, maybe a faint accent. She had great eyes, dark as purple, long-lashed. Griselda hadn't remembered violet eyes. But it was Missy. She remembered the teeth, the look behind the face.

"If these customs men will but hurry." She tapped over to them. She wore black satin pumps with such very high heels. And she had been embracing the Montefierrow twins. That cold something was a lump in Griselda's stomach. It shouldn't be there. Perhaps the twins were Missy's joke.

She returned, spreading her fingers, "*Allons!* It is done. We can go now, Griselda."

"But your luggage?"

"It shall be sent me. At the hotel. I am stopping at the St. Regis."

That great hotel, on the corner across the street. They went into the elevator. "But you can't stay at a hotel alone."

Missy laughed again. "Why not? Because I am *jeune fille?* I have stayed very much at hotels alone. In Paris at the Ritz, in London, at Claridge's…"

Griselda was stern. "But with Maman and her Prince."

Missy shook her head. "But no. Maman is in Rome always. And Rome is so stuffy."

It was Missy who hailed the cab, who directed the driver. Griselda felt an incompetent child with her, as she always felt, with her mother. Missy was too like her.

In the cab, Griselda asked again curiously, trying to make her speech undeliberate, "I still can't see how you knew me. You didn't even know I was in New York."

"Oh, yes, I did."

Griselda waited.

"You know of clipping bureaus? I know all about you and Ann." Missy's grin was a monkey's.

She was startled, amazed. "You don't mean Maman—"

Missy shook her head. "Not Maman. Me." She pounded herself with her fists. Then she was pleading. "You don't mind, Griselda? I had no family. Maman does not want me. And the Prince…" She spat. It wasn't a gesture. It was real. And they were at the St. Regis.

Griselda followed her in, listened to her demand of the clerk certain requirements, a fine suite, with sun, on the corner; listened to him humbly meet the demands. Griselda wondered if she were dreaming again. Desk clerks weren't humble to her; they were snippy. She watched Missy register in a round hand, "Missy Cameron, Palazzio del Artiaggo, Rome, Italy," watched her open her black pouch and dump on the desk a crumpled handful of English notes, a purple lipstick, a powder box shaped like a frog, a knife-thin platinum cigarette case, a stick of chewing gum, a torn white lace handkerchief, and finally a key ring which she shoved at the clerk. "My luggage will arrive. Have it opened and unpacked and cared for." She crammed back the rest of the things.

The clerk said, "Yes, Miss Cameron," and she took a five pound note and handed it to him. "For those who attend the luggage."

She turned back to her sister. "What do we do now?"

"We're going up to Ann's."

She frowned. "So soon? Why do we not go to my rooms first— have a cigarette—an apéritif?"

Griselda refused. She was definite and she didn't know why. She only knew she didn't want to go up to the suite. "Ann is expecting us. She had to take Allen, her little boy, to the dentist. That is why she couldn't meet you."

Missy nodded but she wasn't exactly satisfied. They went out of the door on to Fifty-fifth Street and Griselda didn't say, "I live across the way." She doubted if it would be news anyway. They walked around to Fifth Avenue and hailed a cab.

She said, "Go up Fifth to Seventy-ninth—corner of Seventy-ninth and Madison." Then she turned to Missy. She looked into Missy's eyes and she spoke calmly, spacing her words: "Who were the two young men who met you at the pier?"

Missy's eyes didn't blink. Her voice came surprised. "What two young men? No one met me but you." She opened her bag again, rooted for the cigarette case, took from it a cigarette. It was white with a tiny gold band on the tip, as tiny a gold M monogrammed above it. She asked, "Have you a match, Griselda? You must have seen someone else."

No one else had that mink coat. No one else had icy blonde hair with a circlet of black satin at the back of it. Missy was a liar.

3

Arthur Stepney sat at the head of the dining table. His dark business suit, his starched collar, white shirt, quiet foulard tie, were as uninteresting as his mind. He was good-looking enough, his brown hair beginning to gray at forty, his face tanned from his club sunlamp. He had a face like any other face in a successful bank. It was obvious that Missy thought him dull from the time he came in, gave the correct greeting, suggested the correct sherry, took the most manlike chair in Ann's pale green and ivory living room.

Ann was at the other end of the table, her dark head against the tall period chair. And Griselda saw that Missy didn't like her eldest sister. She was chattery with her. She asked questions but she didn't answer questions except with lies.

Missy liked Griselda, oh, so much! She was sweet; she was childlike; but Griselda understood. Missy didn't like her but she wanted something from her. And that something was mixed up with David and Danny, like as not the something was a mythical very blue marble.

Arthur was beginning to realize and he was duller than ever. "But it is absurd," he said. "Of course you can't stay alone at a hotel. We'll make room for you here. Won't we, Ann?"

Ann looked across the candle flames. "I only wish we could. But we haven't any choice, Arthur, no extra room."

Arthur knew that voice. But he protested, "We can't let her stay alone at a hotel. You know that, Ann. What would my mother think?"

Missy patted his arm. "Please, dear Arthur. Do not be disturbed. I have stayed alone in hotels for these many years."

His eyes opened on her. "I thought on the continent young girls were more protected than here."

She smiled at him. Arthur was susceptible to pretty women and she knew it already. Her hand stayed on his arm.

She said, "The continental girls, yes—but the Americans!" And she told an incident, ever so slightly naughty, about one of the Prince's relatives. They laughed together.

Ann didn't laugh. She rang for Olga and said, "If you were to move to the hotel, Griselda, there would be no question."

Griselda said flatly, "I've no intention of moving to a hotel, Ann. I loathe hotels. I'm lucky to have an apartment here." And to Missy's swift look she added, "I'm sorry I haven't room for you there, but I haven't. I'm only borrowing the apartment anyway and I'd hardly feel like asking anyone else into it. Besides there is no room."

Missy seemed to recognize finality. She shrugged. "Yes, it is too sad, but I have the very fine suite and I like hotels." She was like a small leopard stretching. "I like comfort."

Griselda asked, making her voice light, looking at her endive, "How did you happen to come to New York at this time, Missy?"

"I don't know. I was so tired of Paris, of being alone. I think: I shall come to see my sisters again." Her smile was like a little girl's and her voice.

Griselda insisted, "Did Maman think it a good idea?" She watched but there was no hesitation in Missy's wide eyes.

"But yes. Maman does not care what I do—if I do not bother her." And she laughed again and told Arthur another story, slightly more naughty, about another relative of the Prince.

Ann couldn't ring for Olga now. The salads weren't half eaten. Griselda drew a quick breath. She asked, "Have you ever heard of a blue marble, Arthur?" She was watching under her eyes and she was sure there was some transition behind Missy's mouth.

Arthur was slightly cross at being interrupted. "A blue marble. A blue marble. What kind of a blue marble?"

"I'm sure I don't know. A very blue marble." She included all of them. "Do you know anything about it?"

"I've never heard of anything like that," Ann said.

"How funny!" Missy nibbled her fork.

Arthur said, "What about it?" Griselda put down her fork with a tiny cling against the plate. "Something very strange happened to me last night." Was it last night? It seemed years ago. "I was coming home from the theater. I walked down Fifth and at the corner of Fifty-fifth, two young men spoke to me."

"I hope you didn't speak to them," Ann put in placidly. "It's dangerous. So many things happening these days."

"They were presentable, Ann. I thought college boys at first. And it happened so quickly—and I was frightened…"

"What did you do?" Arthur demanded.

"I couldn't get away. They knew where I lived. I pretended it wasn't the place and tried to walk by but they took my key and they went up with me to the apartment."

Ann's breath was quick. Arthur was frowning. Missy was big-eyed, interested, but there was more. It wasn't for all to see but there was something behind the mask.

"They knew the apartment. They spoke of Con…"

Now Ann was less interested, patronizing again. "Friends of Con, of course." She made it sound as if all friends of Con were expected to do wild, uncouth things.

"I thought so but evidently not. Gig didn't know of them and…" Con couldn't have known them; they'd been abroad twelve years; but she saved that until later, the gossip column. "They fixed drinks and then they said they wanted their marbles, in particular a very blue marble."

"What did you do? Missy asked. She really wanted to know.

Griselda laughed. "Fortunately I didn't have to do anything. Gig arrived just in the nick of time."

"Who's Gig?" Missy asked. The child's face was up again.

"A very brilliant young professor—Columbia-friend of Con's. He lives in the apartment just across the hall."

Ann said, "Well, I must say I think you should move to a hotel. It isn't safe staying where such things can happen."

Griselda spoke slowly, deliberately. "I have no intention of moving to a hotel. I haven't any marbles, and I'm certain Con doesn't keep them. And if he did, he certainly wouldn't leave a valuable one lying around for strange tenants to throw out. He'd put it in a safe or something." Let that message go back. She spoke lightly, "It was probably a joke, and I'm not afraid any more. Not with Gig across the hall. Besides if it were not a joke and they really were looking for a marble, they'll know by now I haven't it."

Missy whooped, "*Quel* excitement! How glad I am that I am in New York!"

Griselda smiled. Then she asked, "Arthur, do you know the Montefierrows here?" This time something did twitch in Missy's temple. She saw it.

"I know the family, of course." He was pompous as always when he knew the great. The Stepneys were not as socially important as they would have liked to be. "The father was chairman of The Bank." The Bank was always Arthur's bank.

Ann was important rather than pompous. "You know my friend, Elizabeth Vandecor. She is a cousin."

Griselda said, "This morning the picture of my two young men was in the *News*. They are the Montefierrow twins—Davidant and Danver. They arrived on Wednesday from Paris."

Ann laughed now and Arthur was relieved. He said, "A prank, of course!" Ann said, "How priceless!" Missy didn't say anything.

Griselda added, "They knew my name and where I lived. I'd never seen them before."

Ann led into the living room. She and Arthur were still pleased with the society joke. They didn't try to explain it. She said, "But we'll have to know them. It's priceless, Griselda."

Griselda asked, "Did you ever meet them in Paris, Missy?"

She looked a petulant child. "I'm only sixteen. I'm not allowed to go out places." It wasn't a lie but it was.

Griselda took a chocolate wafer. "I hope I never have to see them again. It's rather upsetting having such things happen even as a joke."

Ann asked more questions.

Griselda said, "Yes, they're very good-looking. They are twins. Identical twins. But one is dark, the other fair."

She alone knew Missy shivered but it was quickly and the little sister was talking to Arthur about the crossing.

4

Griselda called Gig on the bedroom phone, Ann's crimson and gold bedroom, sitting on one of the crimson coverlets quilted in gold thread. It was only ten o'clock but he was in.

"I've been waiting to hear from you."

She told him, I'm getting ready to leave. I'm at Ann's, my sister's. Take a cab down and I'm going to hide my key in my shoe. I'll ring your bell and you let me in and wait in the upper hall for me."

"Has anything happened today?"

She hesitated. "Not—not exactly."

"I could come for you."

She vetoed that. "I'm not frightened. Only cautious." She told him, "If by any chance you don't hear from me in an hour, ask the superintendent to let you into my apartment, and if I'm not there—start looking."

His voice wobbled. "Maybe I should come get you."

She said, "No," again. "I'll be with my sister. My little sister. She's stopping at the St. Regis. I'll drop her off there. If I'm frightened I'll have a hotel boy walk across with me."

She returned to the living room. The three were still sitting there, Missy in the green brocade chair, Ann in the white, Arthur on the laurel-leaved couch. None was near the foyer phone.

Missy had suggested the leaving before. They all stood in that before-departure apathy. Arthur helped them with coats.

Ann said, "I'll ring you in the morning, Missy. We'll have lunch and make some plans." She seemed only then to realize that none had been made for the youngest. "You'll join us, Griselda?"

She was sorry. She had a business engagement: wholesalers.

She and Missy took the elevator. The doorman whistled the cab, spoke goodnights.

Griselda said, "St. Regis. Go down Madison," and, "I'll drop you there, Missy."

"Where is your lovely apartment?"

You know, she told herself coldly. Aloud she said, "On Fifty-fifth, east, just cat-a-corner from the hotel, nearer Madison."

"I can drop you."

She was definite. "No. I'll see you in and walk across."

Missy extricated the wafer case, lighted another cigarette with the gold M on it. She hadn't smoked at Ann's. This time she had a match. She gurgled, "What fun to be so near. You'll let me see the apartment sometime, won't you?"

Griselda answered, "Of course." She couldn't be uneasy about her own small sister, not too upset.

The cab braked at the hotel. She paid, tipped. She waited while Missy went through the door. She wasn't frightened now; it had gone out of her, and she walked past the bright Western Union office, crossed cornerwise to her apartment, sidling between the cabs parked there, reassured by the squat driver and the thin bruis-er driver arguing on the sidewalk to keep warm. She pushed Gig's bell, keeping her finger on it until she heard the buzzer opening the door. The foyer was deserted as always. There was a momen-tary panic when she opened the heavy door of the elevator but the cage was empty. She felt safe closed in it, pushing number four but-ton. Gig was in the tiny hall, not in pajamas yet, but the old tweed coat, and his warm pipe in his hand.

"All serene?" he queried.

"All serene," she echoed. She was untying her oxford, shak-ing the key out of the right shoe. She handed it to him. While she slid into the shoe, not tieing it, he put the key in the lock, laugh-ing, "What a hiding place!" Then he said queerly as the door was opened, "Better not come in yet, Griselda."

She pushed past him. On the floor, on his back, was a little tubby man with a waxed mustache. Then she knew who it was. Mr. Grain, the superintendent. But she didn't know why he was there in her living room with blood coming out of his vest. All at once she was numb. She couldn't even close her eyes. This was more than fear; it was terror. She didn't think he was there alone. He wasn't.

Danny was in the doorway by the bedroom, his tall silk hat on the back of his blond head, his gold-topped cane under his arm. David closed the door they'd left open. He must have been inside the coat closet. She jumped when the door closed.

David said, "Go right in. A sad accident."

Danny smiled. "Sad. Heart failure."

III

SHE TOOK one step forward and said stupidly, "Heart failure." But it wasn't heart failure. Heart failure didn't mean a river of blood coming out of a man's navel. She looked at Danny. "He's dead. We'll have to call the police." She'd said it just as if he didn't know.

He answered her without moving, "I wouldn't do that."

Gig spoke then. "But we'll have to get the police. It's Mr. Grain. He's dead. I'll call…"

She felt him take one step and stop. David was saying now, "I wouldn't if I were you." She turned slightly. Gig was standing very still. She saw why. David's stick was just touching the tweed coat. In the end of it was the point of a very thin shining thing. Just the point. And David's hand was on the gold knob.

The numb cold went away from her in her sudden fury. She said to one twin, then the other, "You killed him! You killed him!"

Danny was polite. "You mustn't say such things, Griselda."

David spoke as politely, it was to Gig. "You sit on the couch."

Gig walked on eggs, carefully past that dumpy bloody mess, and he sat on the couch. David's stick just touched him. "Stay there. You don't want to get into any trouble."

Gig blinked, "No."

Neither twin came near her. They knew as they had last night that she couldn't open the door and get to the elevator before being stopped. She stood there numbing again, but she was more angry than ever. She said, "You can't murder a man in my apartment and get away with it I'll tell the police. You can't stop me from telling them."

Gig squeaked, "Careful, Griselda."

"I'm not afraid. If they kill me I can't tell, but someone will. They can't murder everyone in New York. And if they don't kill me I'll tell."

Danny's eyes were shiny blue. "We have no intention of killing you, Griselda. What an idea!"

David was lighting a cigarette. "You don't want to make a fool of yourself, Griselda. What would you tell the police?"

She was wrathful. "That you killed Mr. Grain. That you—"

Now Danny lit his cigarette. "We say it's heart failure."

"But it isn't heart failure! People don't bleed from heart failure!" They were making sport of her and suddenly from her weakness she wanted to cry. That made her more angry.

David smiled at her. "Maybe it isn't heart failure. But you mustn't blame us for what happens in Con's apartment. Oh, don't distress yourself, Griselda! We won't leave him littering up your charming room. We'll take care of him."

Danny said, "But I shouldn't think of speaking to the police if I were you, Griselda. What if they went after Con? It is his apartment, you know."

Her heart stopped beating. The police couldn't go after Con. Con wasn't here. He had nothing to do with this. But—it was his apartment. And if he weren't really gone? If he were pretending to be away? That was ridiculous! But she remained stone, knowing something with certainty. He was safely away from this horror. She couldn't wouldn't ever, bring him back into it. It didn't matter what the twins or anyone did to her. No one should touch Con.

Danny continued, "It is so simple. We came in and found him lying there. I'm sure the police would believe our story."

She asked, "How would you explain breaking into my apartment?"

Danny was still laughing, "But we didn't break in, Griselda. You gave us a key and told us to meet you here." He was twirling a door key in his hand. "Of course, we'd hate to name you…"

She felt weak all at once, as if she'd have to sit down. David was there with the chair. She shook her head slowly from side to side. "I don't know what to believe. Whether you are criminals, or—"

David finished, "—gentlemen adventurers."

She stared at him. "I suppose you're still after the same thing."

David's eyes were dark as wells. "The very blue marble."

And then someone was opening the backstairs door, that always bolted door. She jumped up, her voice caught, soundless. She was shaking. Danny swung in the doorway and his cane was pointed to where her eyes had stared. She sank down again, stupefied. Missy was standing there.

2

Missy didn't see her or anyone. She saw the fat bloody suit on the floor. She looked at Danny. "Fool!" she cried. "You fool!"

Danny struck her across the mouth hard with the back of his hand. "Keep quiet!"

Griselda shivered back into the chair. David's fingers were an almost unfelt pressure on her shoulder.

Missy rubbed her mouth as a child would. Her violet eyes were on Danny and Griselda felt sick. David said to Missy, his fingers still on Griselda, "Why did you come here?"

She spoke as if her mouth were raw. "I knew you'd get into trouble if I didn't watch you."

Danny told her, "We're in no trouble. Heart failure."

She began to laugh then and Danny laughed too. Then he leaned over and kissed her eyebrow. "Get some towels and a blanket."

Gig hadn't said a word. Now he spoke pathetically, as if he were in an insane asylum and trying to be tactful. "If you'd let me have a match, I'd smoke my pipe."

"But of course." David passed him a box from the desk.

Danny took the blanket and rolled that figure into its hammock. "Clean the mess," he said. Missy was on her knees scrubbing with the wet towels, Con's towels.

David spoke. "We'll take the soiled things, Griselda, and the rug. We'll send fresh ones tomorrow. You don't mind."

She couldn't speak. She was watching her little sister, mink coat spread behind her like a ballet dress, scrubbing blood from a polished floor. Danny had pulled the blanket through the bedroom doorway and into the back hall outside. He came in again. "Give me the towels," he said.

Missy stood up and handed them to him. He flung them into the hall and he took the rug away. He said, "Missy will watch until we return." He handed her his stick. David crossed to his side and they went out the back way.

Missy stood in Danny's place in the doorway. Griselda didn't move. She didn't speak until after the door was closed for two or three minutes. Then she said, "You told me you didn't know them."

Missy yawned. "Fool. You knew I did."

Gig spoke crossly, as if he didn't like any of this. "Who is that, Griselda?"

She laughed, hysteria in that laugh. "I forgot my manners, I'm afraid. My sister, Missy Cameron—Dr. Gigland."

Missy said, "I've heard of you. You're Gig."

"Yes. How do you do."

He started to rise and she said as if she were bored:

"The twins' sticks are so clever. This end there's a lovely little sword, a very fine two-edged one, easy to release. You press here"—she put a finger on the place under the knob but she didn't press—"and it jumps out. Then up here if you press, there's gas—not fatal—just rather stupefying. That's only for a tight place, of course. Then if you twist the knob and push here," she displayed the place, her boredom gone, her face screwed with interest, "it locks the sword and releases a dart. Poisoned, of course, but a quick poison."

Gig nodded. "Very interesting." He was down in place again.

Griselda couldn't speak.

"An African made them—of course the twins helped him with the designing."

Griselda asked, "How long have you known them—the twins?"

"I met them the first year that Maman and I went over. They visited us at the Villa that summer. But I've only lived with them for three years, two really. The first year didn't count. I was staying with Cousin Paulina in Paris and supposed to be going to school. It was made difficult."

Gig asked, "How old is your sister?"

Griselda answered. "Sixteen." Passionately, she wanted to know, "Why do you stay with them? They're evil—dangerous. Don't you know they're evil?"

Missy's dark eyes flickered but she asked easily, "Do you think so? I think they're sweet." Her eyes were even darker. She looked straight at Griselda. "Danger is sweet."

Gig said, just as if Missy weren't there, "I'm afraid your sister is a psychopathic case, Griselda."

She moved her head. "I don't know. I don't understand anything."

Missy pursed her lips. "I do not think you are being very nice to me, Herr Gig." She laughed. "Can you not see it is just a game?"

His voice was soft to her. "Murder isn't a game."

Her eyebrows darted. "Murder? Murder? But it was heart failure! You heard the twins say heart failure."

Griselda spoke without hope. "I suppose you know about the marble. Is it asking too much that you tell me about it?"

Missy shrugged. "You will have to ask the twins. All I know—there is a marble."

"But..." Griselda broke off again to that back door opening. The twins came in. They double-bolted the door. Danny took his cane, patted Missy's head. "No trouble, baby?"

She lifted her shoulders sadly, "No trouble."

David came into the room. "Nor had we. Everything is safe. You needn't worry, Griselda." He bent over her in the chair. "But you will think twice before you call the police. Believe me, it will not do any good—to anyone." She met his eyes. They were dark, beautiful, but you couldn't see into them. She didn't answer.

Missy opened the door. The twins tilted their hats with their sticks. "Goodnight, Griselda. See you soon." They left the door open, the sticks pointed towards it until the elevator arrived. Danny closed it then; you could hear the bolts catch. And you could hear the elevator going down.

For a moment Griselda thought she was going to be sick. Then anger surged. "I'm not going to stand this, Gig. It's intolerable. It's unbelievable. These things don't happen." She walked swiftly over to the windows, avoiding that spot where the small rug had been. She flung one window wide, leaned out, looking below. She saw them come out of the apartment house. They hailed a cab. They were laughing when they entered it. She closed the window with a thump and turned. "We've got to do something."

Gig was yet on the couch, coddling his pipe. He agreed. "Yes. But what can we do? I think they've tied our hands. They've removed the body, cleaned the place. We shouldn't have let them."

She asked, "What should we have done—taken the poison, the gas, or just the sword?" Then she was sorry for speaking to him out of her anger for others. She said, "I'm going to have a drink, will you?"

He sounded surprised at himself. "I believe I will." He looked at his watch. "I must get some sleep tonight." He was unbelieving. "It lacks twenty to midnight." She too was amazed, the night had been as months, or aeons.

They sat side by side on the couch with the drinks.

"Will you want me to stay here tonight?"

She didn't know if he wished it or feared it. She said she wouldn't. "I'm not afraid of them now. They're real to me. Missy is my own sister. They can't hurt me. I don't have their old marble."

He drank. "If Missy were my sister, I'd get her out of what she's in quickly."

"I wish I could."

He insisted, "You're certain you know nothing about the marble?"

"I don't know why they should even think I know anything about it."

Something occurred to her. Gig might communicate with Con, try to bring him home to take care of things. He mustn't do that Con must be kept out at all costs. She added casually, "I don't want Con to know about this. It's an important assignment he has, covering this border affair for N.B.C. There's no reason to bother him."

He agreed. "No." He set away his glass. "I'll say goodnight. You're certain you don't want me to stay."

She repeated, "I'm not afraid. But I think I shall always call you before I start home nights after this."

He turned at the door. "If I'm not in?"

"Then I won't come home alone. I'll bring someone with me."

He thought that was wise. He hesitated. She knew he would

stay given a word. It wasn't that she didn't wish it. He wasn't Con but he was nice and he wanted to stay. She didn't know why she didn't speak.

3

After he had gone the room was too quiet. She snapped on the radio that there might be a cessation of the silence and peace but she had been wrong. She twisted the dial to a late news broadcast and suddenly Con was in the room; out of that non-committal box, Con's deep, dear voice came. She was aching with her need of him and his voice was there but she couldn't answer back; couldn't tell him all she must tell him; she could only listen to that voice discussing the trivialities of border trouble.

She silenced the room again quickly. Then she looked carefully at the bolted door and turned out the living room lights. Quickly she moved to the bedroom, closed the Venetian blinds and undressed. It steadied her to cream her face, wipe away the cream, pat astringent, begin brushing her golden hair.

If Aunt Charlotte knew she'd be on the next plane flying East. She considered with comfort her aunt's domineering nose, her brook-no-nonsense shoulders. But she couldn't send for Aunt Charlotte. If she came, and if Con returned, there wouldn't be a chance to... She put down the brush. To what, she didn't know.

If Con had the marble... Until tonight she hadn't thought of it as a marble. Long ago, when they were first married, that little blue jewel. It had somehow frightened her even then; she didn't know where he had picked it up, but she hadn't wanted it in his possession. Con had laughed at her and had said once, "Wouldn't the police like to know I have this." After that she didn't see it again.

And Missy, too, had seen it. She recalled now. Before the little sister had sailed with Maman. Missy had wanted it, her eyes greedy on it that afternoon in the apartment when Con came in, found her toying with it. But Missy couldn't have remembered that long ago. It had been only an incident and she had been a child.

Why was it so important? No one would fling a really valuable thing around in an apartment. Of course it wasn't here. If Con did still possess it, it would be in a vault, some place safe. No one would be fool enough to carry it with him or hide it carelessly where any marauder might search it out. No one but Con. He had no sense about such things.

If she could find it, get rid of it for him, it would keep him safe. She must keep him safe. The twins had evidently failed in their search here for it; surely she had no chance. Yet perhaps they had not searched as yet; perhaps they had been interrupted. And they didn't know the little secrets she and Con had shared.

She was ready for bed. She knew where to look, the grinning Golliwog perfume bottle on the chest. She had thought perhaps Con kept it all these years for sentimental reasons, because it had been hers. Con sentimental! She lifted the Golliwog's head, pointed the dark stopper to her chin. Hidden in her hands she knew where to turn the head, no one else would know.

It had been faulty. He had hollowed it and once he had left little rolled-up balls of paper there with messages to her, when he went early on an assignment and she lay still asleep in their bed. Their hollow tree. She hoped the marble wouldn't be there.

It was such a tiny blue ball, blue as cloisonné is blue. She had forgotten its beauty. She put it in the drawer among the handkerchiefs. If anyone had searched they had surely already rummaged there. Tomorrow she would think of a safe place for it. She couldn't just throw it away after all; it was Con's; he might want it again.

She replaced the perfume stopper, climbed into bed, snapped

off the lamp. She was almost asleep when her throat began to prickle with fear. She had remembered careless words, "No trouble." She was certain now that Missy would have welcomed trouble. Missy had wanted to use that lethal cane.

IV

BETTE WAS Saturday cleaning, moving furniture, spreading that nice-smelling polish on the floor. Griselda looked at the clock. Ten-fifteen. She called, "Bette."

"Yes, Miss." Soft-spoken, sweet-faced, she was in the door.

"Would you be an angel? Hand me my juice and the coffee. I'm lazy."

Bette's smile was twinkles. "Yes, indeed, Miss."

She thinks I've been on a party. "And the papers," she called.

Bette brought them. Her smile liked serving a pretty woman in bed. Good as the pictures it was. She handed over the glasses case without being asked. Then she was the cleaner again. "Did you know the little rug's not in the living room?"

Griselda opened the paper, shut her face away. "Yes. Someone spilled—a drink—on it last night. He took it to be cleaned."

Bette understood parties. She worked for Con. She said, "I hope the stain will come out. Sometimes they're hard to get out." She returned to the polishing.

Griselda drank her juice, turning pages of the paper. There they were again in the tabloid. "Old friends of the continent meet in Manhattan. Montefierrow twins and companion tour night spots." Missy, of course. "Missy Cameron, daughter of the Princess del Artiaggio of Rome, Italy, and the late Dr. T. W. Cameron of Park Avenue, who arrived yesterday on the *Queen Mary*, toured the Manhattan night spots with the Montefierrow twins last night. The picture taken in the Stork Club…" And so on. No mention of Hollywood's Griselda Cameron Satterlee, thank God. She had a distaste of publicity amounting almost to mania. The heart break of her divorce and her picture slathered in the tabs, knowing how Con must have writhed with his newspaperman's scorn of such things. And after that the movies, all the tawdry stunts the studio had done on the front pages to build her, she too numb then to care. Always publicity beating against her name. She had only been a little girl but she would never forget her father's sick eyes in the newspaper when her mother divorced him. She wouldn't let it soil her again. She'd stay away from the twins. No mention of Mrs. Arthur Stepney of East Seventy-ninth Street either. Ann would be annoyed.

The phone. She was afraid to answer but it was Ann.

"Have you seen the *News?* Olga brought her copy to me. Missy's picture with those fascinating twins you were telling about. She said she didn't know them, you know…"

"Yes, I know."

"But it seems she did. She just didn't know our pronunciation. Isn't that amusing? The Italian of their name is so different. She told me what it was. Are you meeting us for lunch?"

"I can't, you recall."

"Oh, yes. Dinner?"

"I'm so sorry." She couldn't face Missy. Not until she knew what to do. "I'm afraid I can't make it."

"I'm so sorry too. Missy has promised to try to bring the twins. At any rate you'll come for cocktails tomorrow afternoon, just a few intimates to meet Missy. Bring Gig if you wish."

She got rid of Ann. So her sister had taken up the young one. But of course. For society Ann would do anything. But what if she knew the truth? She wouldn't believe it Missy and the twins could out-lie any truth-tellers.

Bette said at the door, "Miss Satterlee, poor Mrs. Grain, the wife of the superintendent you know, is so worried. Mr. Grain went out about nine o'clock last night to see about something and he's not back yet. You didn't see him, did you, Miss Satterlee?"

She didn't look at the maid. She swallowed trying to make words come. She had to speak false ones that must sound false. Not for herself, for Con. Keep him from danger. Her voice to her was surprisingly even. "Why, no, Bette. I had dinner at my sister's and didn't return here until after ten. Then some friends came in."

Bette half-apologized for being presumptuous. "I didn't think you would have, Miss. I only asked because I found this under the couch." Griselda didn't move. She was frozen. "It's that penny he always carried on his watch chain, his lucky penny—"

Griselda turned in the bed. Her eyes were wide. Bette had the coin on her hand. "Are you certain it's the same one, Bette?"

"Oh, yes, Miss." She was as serious as a nun, holding the copper coin. "It's a foreign one, Mex he called it. It's bigger than our pennies, you see, and that little hole in it—see? I'd know it anywhere."

Griselda saw. She wondered if Bette knew how hard it was to keep her face real. She repeated, "I didn't see him." Words, stupid words. "He must have dropped it here some other time." That wasn't right. "I wonder how long it's been there." That was wrong.

The woman said, "He was never without it. I was behind that couch Wednesday, Miss Satterlee, it must have been since then. Maybe he brought in a package last night before you come home."

She answered, "There was no package. I didn't see any," and knew again she had spoken wrong words.

Bette kept turning the coin. "Shall I give it to Mrs. Grain, Miss?"

"Please." She couldn't stay in bed, in this apartment. "Tell her if I can help in any way—"

"That's good of you. She don't know where he could have gone. He's never stayed away all night in the forty years they been married. A steady man, Miss. There's not many of them." Then she turned abruptly and went out, slipping the coin in her pocket.

She didn't suspect anything, Griselda knew. She was worried about the poor man, and his wife sleeping alone after forty years. He would never sleep with her again. He—but she didn't know where he was. Maybe he'd never be found again. Only his lucky coin would be found. She was trembling in the hot shower. If the lucky coin hadn't rolled away would his luck have held? She'd join Ann and Missy for dinner if the twins would be there. She'd find out. They couldn't do this, let her in for it.

2

She dressed quickly. It looked dank out, grim. She put a clean handkerchief with a round thing inside it into her bag. She sat on the edge of the bed, ruffled the hotels, dialed.

"I should like to speak to Missy Cameron." She held the wire. She was afraid Missy would be out but she wasn't. "This is Griselda."

"Griselda." Missy's voice sounded as if she'd never heard the name.

"Are the twins dining with you tonight? With Ann and Arthur?"

"Why?"

Griselda spoke with impact. "I must see them. If you are all dining together I will join you. Otherwise I won't."

Missy said, "Wait."

The wire was quiet. Griselda was nervous, her back to that double-bolted back door. She turned on the bed to keep it visible. No need to be frightened with Bette cleaning in the next room.

Missy's voice said, "You could see them now."

"I couldn't. I've a business engagement. Will they be at dinner tonight?"

Without hesitation came the answer, "They will."

"Tell Ann I'll join you. I'll find out where later."

Missy suggested, "We'll call for you."

She was cold. "I'd rather not. I'll speak to Ann later." She rang off, went into the living room. "I'm going now, Bette." She laid the week's money on the mantelpiece. She couldn't help repeating, "Tell Mrs. Grain I'll help in any way."

"Yes, Miss. Like as not he'll be back before long." She leaned on the mop handle. "Maybe an accident. She's been calling the hospitals."

She had to say it, was surprised that she urged it. "And the police—of course, the police."

Bette said, "She don't want to call in the police, Miss. Not unless there's a need to. She don't want to be in the papers. They're decent people, never had any trouble—and it gives the apartment a bad name, the police."

"Yes." She went out, leaving the door ajar until the elevator came. No one seemed to want the police. Except herself. And she couldn't call them. Not now. Not and risk having them go after Con; worse, set the twins after Con.

It was relief to be bouncing downtown, out of that neighborhood. It was joy to meet Joie Eisenhorn with his bristle jowls and spats, to finger velvets of candy colors, jewel-smooth satins, starchy brocades. Lunch in a noisy unheard-of restaurant with strange, Kosher foodstuffs was reality. And then it was time to return to fear.

She walked up Fifth, stopping at Best's, thinking of Ann's Cornelia, kept in with threatening weather and a cold. She saw a doll, golden yarn curls, pink organdie ruffles. It was a Cornelia doll. "I want this."

She carried the package. On up the Avenue. The new Kresge's. A fascinating place to dally, and always things needed at the ten cent store. She stopped at one counter, needles, thread. She remembered, more ash trays for the apartment. She bought heavy chain locks; at least when she was inside at night no one could enter. She could get up mornings and let Bette in.

Now she had too many bundles. And she would have to find something for Allen. She couldn't take presents to Cornelia and not to Allen. She crossed the street, took a Fifth bus to Schwartz's. A lovely game with marbles—not marbles, no! There was a barnyard, better. And a funny tiny stuffed donkey Nana would adore for a pincushion. Laden she went out, hailed a cab. "Seventy-ninth and Madison."

Olga told her, "Mrs. Stepney is at the masseuse. The children are asleep, I believe."

She handed her coat and hat to the maid. "I'll be in Mrs. Stepney's room. Tell Nana to let me know when the children wake. I've presents."

Safe behind Ann's bedroom door. The twins wouldn't bother Ann; they didn't want anything here. With nail scissors she ripped a seam. The tiny blue ball into the very center of the cotton-stuffed doll. Replace the rip with tiny matching stitches. No one would ever know; no one would dream. After this was over, as soon as the twins realized she didn't have it and went away, she could return it to Con. No one would touch the doll until then; Cornelia at two years was jealous of her possessions.

Three o'clock. Ann wouldn't return until four. The babies would probably sleep that long on a park-less day. She had time to relax.

3

Dinner in the Persian Room. Ann, lovely, correct, masseused, in Mainbocher because of Her Royal Highness, sherry satin with something white shocking it. Arthur, knife-pleated in tails. The twins, uniforms of tails. Missy in pale lemon chiffon, Alix of course, color of her hair. You wouldn't think it was becoming but it was; everyone in the room looking at her. Griselda in black sheer, daring cut, startling, her own model.

David said, "It's strange how different three sisters can be, and how separately beautiful and distinguished." He and Danny were any two young men about town, well bred, educated, monied. They had accepted introductions to Griselda.

Ann asked, "What do you mean?" Her eyes challenged, languorous. She was between Danny and Arthur, Griselda on Arthur's left between him and David. Missy, of course, between the twins.

Missy spoke rather crossly, "David's always being poetic. I want to dance." She caught Danny's hand and they danced as if they were sculptured together.

Ann was eyeing David. Griselda said to him, "I'd like to dance, too." Ann didn't like it when they moved together.

She didn't want to be close to him but she had to talk. "My cleaning woman found the superintendent's lucky charm under the couch."

He was surprisingly angry. His face was dark as shadows. He was exclaiming but not to her. "Stupidity! That's what comes of hurrying. *Stupide! Stupide!*" He remembered her there in his arms. "And what did you say?"

She recited.

"That's what comes of hurrying. He is always impatient. Have you told him?"

"Who? Danny?"

The music had stopped. They walked so slowly back to the table. "Yes."

"I haven't told anyone. I haven't seen anyone. I only came here tonight to tell you about it. I didn't want to come. I didn't want to see any of you again. Murder—"

He laughed gently. "You still think we killed him."

Then they were at the table, seated again.

Ann laughed, not too kindly. She had been waiting for the moment: "Griselda, why did you pretend you didn't know the boys? You surely have had more than the one meeting with them."

If Ann had been wise, she would have noticed how Danny, how Missy, how David, how Griselda all looked quickly at her. Maybe she did notice. Maybe even dull Arthur did. Her laugh was less real.

"Griselda told us about you joining her the other evening. Such a priceless thing!"

"Wasn't it?" Danny laughed. He looked at Griselda without any expression.

She was afraid. She wanted to make it definite what she had repeated. Her laugh was nervous. "Yes, I was telling about it at dinner last night."

Arthur came in from his fog. "What about this marble you were talking about? What was all that about?"

Nobody said anything. It was only for a moment but it was stark. Griselda shivered when David spoke, spoke so easily, so sweetly.

"You mean the very blue marble?" He leaned slightly across Griselda to Arthur and she could see his pulse beating in his throat.

Arthur was hearty. "I suppose it was a blue one. I don't remember. Griselda seemed to think it was important. Sounds silly to me."

Missy had lighted a cigarette, one with a small gold M. She

said, "It is important." Her mouth was something harsh and her eyes frightening, like the twins', without expression. "If Griselda would but give us the marble we would go away."

Danny said under his breath, "Quiet," and David, "Too late!" But Danny added aloud, "What Missy says is true."

Ann was troubled; she wasn't that stupid. Arthur, always the host, laughed, "Then I hope she won't give it to you. We'd hate to have you leave just when you've arrived. Wouldn't we, Ann?" But he broke off, uncertain, seeing Ann's face, looking now at the others.

Ann whispered, "Why don't you give it to them?"

Griselda spoke to Danny's face, "I don't have it. And if I did I wouldn't give it to you. You know why." Then she remembered; she was safe, in the Persian Room, ordinary surroundings. She could be normal, herself. "What makes you think I have it? What makes you think I know anything about it?"

David said, "It was in Con Satterlee's hands. He's had it—how long we do not know. But we have definitely traced it to him. We came at once but he was gone."

Griselda told him. It was as if no one else was at the table. "I was Con's wife for three years. I have been divorced from him for four years. I haven't seen him in four years. Why don't you get it from Con?"

David answered, "He doesn't have it now. It isn't with him on the border."

"How do you know?"

"He has been searched."

She was cold. She spoke absurdly, eagerly, "Maybe he left it some place on the way."

"He didn't stop on the way. He flew out."

"Maybe he gave it to the pilot—to someone…"

"It is too important to give away." His head bowed just a little as he spoke.

Arthur was impatient. "Why is it so important? Marbles aren't so important. What's there about this particular one?"

Danny and David and Missy looked at each other. Griselda watched them. Danny was spokesman. He was angling for words, words that would not say much.

"The blue marble belongs to us. It was stolen from us five years ago. It isn't really a marble, you see; it looks like one. It contains something important to us. That is why we want it."

Arthur was literal. "If it's something belongs to you I don't see why you don't just ask Con for it instead of searching his things and that sort of stuff. Con wouldn't keep something that didn't belong to him. Would he, Griselda?"

She said no, then she smiled half at David, half at Arthur. "Maybe it's one of those Finders Keepers things. Maybe it did belong to the twins and now it belongs to Con."

David's eyes were glittery. "Maybe," he admitted. But Danny was angry, hiding it but angry. "You're wrong, Griselda. We came by the marble honestly."

David laughed now. "Yes, we traded a cabin plane, two-seater, perfectly good except petrol-less and a broken wheel, for it."

They had Arthur on their side again. "Must be a pretty valuable curio to you."

"It is—to us."

Griselda baited, "To no one else?"

David shrugged, "I do not know why it should be to anyone else."

She said, "Then Con wouldn't want it. He probably doesn't even know he has it." Her eyes narrowed, "Why is it so valuable to you?"

Missy broke in, "What does it matter? It isn't yours. Why don't you give it to us?"

Griselda asked blandly, "How do you come into it, Missy?"

The girl was furious. Dan put his fingers about her upper arm.

David smiled, "Missy is our *petite amie*." Danny said, "She is one-third of us."

Missy started to say something but she didn't have a chance.

Someone shrieked in a too British accent, "Griselda, my dear! Griselda Satterlee!" She bent over Griselda, leaving her young man posing foolishly alone. It was Nesta Fahney, not on the screen, in person, but with the double length eyelashes, the crimson mouth, the porcelain teeth, the daring cream lace gown embroidered in real gardenias. "But, Griselda, this is too fortunate. I didn't know where you were and you must dress me! I'm going to London next week and I must be dressed!"

Griselda told her, "I've no one here to work for me."

"But, darling, your taste! You must shop with me."

Griselda introduced, "My sister, Mrs. Stepney, Mr. Stepney, Miss Fahney." She remembered Missy was a sister, too. "And my younger sister, Miss Cameron, Miss Fahney. The Messrs. Monte-fierrow."

She knew now. Nesta had come over to meet the twins, not to be dressed. But she would probably insist on that too. She turned in her chair, "Hello, Jasper." She introduced the beautiful hero, "Jasper Coldwater."

Arthur was heavy with delight. "You must join us, Miss Fahney." He gave up his chair, beckoned for more. Ann smiled her best at Jasper. The other three didn't know the idols of the American screen. They didn't care for the interruption but the twins were polite and Missy finally stared at Jasper. Nesta sat by Arthur but she batted eyelashes at the twins.

"You will shop with me, Griselda? I haven't a stitch. And for London…"

Danny was charming. "London isn't particular in these times, Miss Fahney." He didn't pronounce her name just right. He stood, "This is my dance, Griselda."

She didn't want to. She was sewed to her chair. But he came over, offered his arm and Nesta's eyes sighed.

They danced. He said, "Why did you tell those people of the marble? It would be better if they were out of it. Too many are in it now. What did you say of last night?"

"Nothing," she answered truthfully. "But I will tell you something. Mr. Grain, the man you murdered, always wore a lucky coin on his watch chain. My maid found it under my couch this morning."

He didn't speak but she could feel his muscles twitch. She repeated all that she had told David.

Finally he said, "You need not worry about this. If you keep quiet you will get in no trouble."

The music halted, began again. They danced silently. The number was over. He asked, standing in front of her there on the floor, "Why were you asking all the questions about the marble? You know about it. Don't you?"

She looked straight at him. "No, I don't."

V

BETTE DIDN'T come on Sundays. But at nine o'clock someone was pounding at the door, pounding hard. Griselda came out of sleep, belted her white robe about her, put her feet into the white cord slippers, and went to answer. She opened it on the chain. She saw the uniform, and another man not in uniform.

The uniform said, "Sorry to disturb you, Miss. We'd like to ask a few questions if you don't mind."

"One moment." The door had to be shut to take off the chain. She could close her eyes for that space, try to think. She opened the door. "You'll excuse how I look. I was asleep." Then she asked, "What's happened?"

The policeman was Sergeant Moore; the plainclothes man, Inspector Tobin. They told her their names after Tobin had asked, "You're Mrs. Satterlee?"

"I use Miss." Such a trivial correction. Then she repeated. "What's happened? You've found him?"

Tobin's nostrils twitched. Moore stared at her.

"Found whom?"

"Mr. Grain, the superintendent."

The Inspector had eyes that could look sideways. His mouth was sideways, too. "What do you know about it?"

She had spoken too quickly but she could make it right. "My maid told me." She walked to a chair, motioned for them to be seated. She skirted the new rug but they walked right where he had been, not dead of heart failure.

"Where is she?"

They sat on the couch. The Sergeant's knees were in his way. He took off his cap, awkwardly. The Inspector didn't remove his brown fedora.

"She doesn't come on Sundays. She told me yesterday morning. Mrs. Grain was worried." She repeated that pathetic little quirk. "He hadn't been away from her at night for forty years." She felt her nostrils sting as if tears were coming. Ridiculous, yet it was sad. She asked again, "You've found him?"

"Yeah." The Inspector answered out of his mouth.

She leaned forward but she took a cigarette before speaking. She looked at the match and her voice sounded natural. "Where?"

"The janitor found him."

"Janitor?" Her eyes widened.

Sergeant Moore said, "Certainly knocked him for a loop."

She repeated. She had to know. "Where was he—when the janitor found him?"

The Inspector asked, "D'ya mind, Miss?" He took a battered pack of Luckies from his pocket.

She urged, "Forgive me, I forgot." She handed her box across, insisted. She laughed a little. "I don't know the manners of an investigation. I've never been in one."

He laughed too, not very much. "Don't imagine you have. You're visiting, aren't you?"

"Yes."

"Your husband's apartment?"

"Yes, he offered it to me. He's away. We are divorced, you know."

He seemed to know. He pushed his hat sideways. "Yeah. Sort of a funny setup, isn't it?"

Her eyes widened again, deliberately now. She didn't know

where he was heading. "You mean my using this place?" She shook her head, thinking it out. "No. No, it isn't. I haven't seen him in four years but it's like him to offer. He read in the paper that I was coming, and wrote offering…"

"You write letters to each other then?" The Sergeant asked this.

"No. I don't imagine we've written a half dozen in that time. Always for business reasons. But—if you knew my former husband, you'd understand."

Inspector Tobin turned his lip in. "I know him."

She was surprised but insisted, "You understand then. It's like him. Generous, and matter-of-fact." She didn't know why it mattered to them.

"Yeah." He was fiddling with his hands now and she saw what was there, the copper coin.

She nodded at it. "Bette found it under this couch Saturday morning. She knew it was Mr. Grain's, his lucky piece. That is how she came to tell me that he was missing."

The Inspector tossed it. "Yeah. You had a party here Friday night."

She was doing well, calm, natural. "Not exactly that. I was at dinner at my sister's, uptown. Mrs. Arthur Stepney. Arthur is a vice-president of Madison National."

He inserted the inevitable, "Yeah," and the Sergeant said, "That's the bank at Forty-second and Madison," as if someone didn't know.

"Yes. Some friends dropped in after my return. It wasn't really a party."

Tobin questioned, "Names?"

"Names." She hadn't understood at first, then she did. "Professor Gigland, a friend of Con's. His apartment is across the hall. Teaches at Columbia." She hesitated the barest second but she couldn't make up names. They'd be checked. Sergeant Moore's eyes were memorizing. "David and Danny Montefierrow." That surprised them. She knew it although they said nothing. "And my younger sister, Missy Cameron."

The Sergeant asked, "Is she staying with you?"

"No. She's at the St Regis. She lives in Rome with my mother."

"Yeah."

If there were only something to say, some way to say it, to make them believe truth. She had wanted the police. She had them now and she wasn't saying a word. She couldn't. The twins had warned.

The Inspector turned the coin. "You think maybe Grain lost this under the couch sometime? Think it's been there long? Before Con left maybe?" He was looking at the coin but at her too.

"It couldn't have been there long. Bette is a thorough cleaner. She'd cleaned earlier in the week."

"Think maybe someone dropped it Friday night?"

The question came so quickly her mouth opened, stupid as an idiot child's. She hadn't considered that as an explanation. She'd thought they must know Grain had been here, lying there, on that spotless rug. She answered truthfully, "That never occurred to me."

The Sergeant put in, "Have you known these folks long?" It seemed as if he sensed things, as if he could see the picture on the back of her mind.

"You mean my guests?"

"Yeah."

"My sister, naturally." She smiled. "Although I haven't seen her since she was a child. Gig—Professor Gigland—I met only when I came here, and the twins very recently. They are friends of Missy's, my sister, from abroad." She took a breath. "I know of course that Mr. Grain is dead."

"You do?" His eyes popped at her.

She flung out her hands. "I know he must be. You wouldn't be here otherwise." She said thoughtfully, truthfully, "I knew he was dead when Bette told me. After forty years he wouldn't have stayed away from his wife otherwise."

"I guess not," Moore agreed. "Though some would." He grinned.

Inspector Tobin asked, "Did you see Grain Friday?"

"Friday night?"

"Any time Friday."

"No, not that day." She bit her lip. "I saw him the day I arrived. He had the key for me and helped me in with my bags. And one or two noons he was out front when I went out." She added irrelevantly, wondering what the wife was like. "I've never seen her."

The front buzzer had been touched. Tobin said, "I'll answer." He walked to the entrance button, pushed it, not answering the house phone.

He waited to open the door. Moore was still at the windows, looking out. He wanted to know, "There wouldn't be no reason for him to be in your apartment Friday, would there? Before you came home?"

"No. Not unless he brought a package. But I hadn't sent any and there was none here." She swirled in the chair as the bell rang.

Tobin opened the door. David Montefierrow was smiling there.

2

"Griselda! I didn't know you were busy."

He did know. Somehow he knew. He came purposely; and he looked handsome and gay, normal, in morning clothes. Of course, his inevitable stick.

She was pleased to say, "David, this is Inspector Tobin. Sergeant Moore. David Montefierrow."

Tobin closed the door.

David put his bowler, his gray gloves, his stick, his topcoat, on a chair. He came over and took her hand. "Police. Don't tell me you've been shoplifting." He laughed heartily.

She took away her hand. "They have found Mr. Grain."

"No?" He was completely surprised. "The missing superintendent? Griselda told us last night how worried her char was." He took Tobin's place on the couch, lighted one of his special cigarettes and asked, "What was it? Amnesia? Or an accident?" He was politely curious, not very interested.

Moore said, "The janitor found him. In the basement. Back of the trunk lockers."

David asked, "What had happened?"

"Looks as if he plugged himself in the stomach."

Griselda leaned to the words. David was so at ease. "Really?"

Tobin said, "Yeah. Gun was there on the floor. A thirty-eight, new one. Must have bought it purposely. Only his wife says he didn't have any reason for suicide."

"Better off than they've been in years," Moore continued. "Good job, owners liked him, no debts, good health. No worry she knew of."

David asked with the right interest, "Does she think it was murder? Why would he be murdered?"

Griselda wanted to scream, to have to sit here, listen to this, and to know. She stood. "I'm going to put some coffee on. I can't go any longer without it. You'll all have some." She went into the kitchen cubby.

She could hear Moore answer, "He didn't have any money on him, no valuables, and nothing missing. Except that lucky piece."

Inspector Tobin said, "If it weren't for finding that here—and there wasn't much blood—it'd be open and shut suicide."

David spoke casually, "Of course, he dropped it here. Probably came in, say, to inspect a leak, or lights or something, whatever it is these supers do, and caught his chain. He wore it on his watch chain, the maid told Griselda. Probably didn't even notice it was gone until later, and didn't know where he'd lost it."

Griselda with the cups was in time to see his delighted smile, a little daring now.

"Maybe that's why he popped himself off, lost his lucky piece."

They all laughed. She didn't. She set down the cups and went back for the coffee, the cream and sugar.

They all drank coffee. It was friendly. When they had finished she said, "You'll excuse me if I go dress. I've a lunch engagement at one, with Nesta Fahney." She mentioned the name purposely to interest the police. The noon bells were ringing from St. Patrick's. "If you're finished with me." She smiled at them.

"Yes, indeed, Mrs.—Miss Satterlee," Moore said.

David asked, "Shall I drop you at Nesta's hotel, Griselda?"

She told him no. "I don't want to keep you."

She thought the police were leaving. David also thought so. But they closed him out easily. Inspector Tobin told her, "You won't mind if we look around."

"Naturally not."

She shut herself into the bedroom. She didn't want the temptation of peeking at what they were about to do. She dressed quickly, she was late, the black satin with the scattered silver pin points in it, black furs and hat again. She put on her glasses. No need to strain her eyes for Nesta Fahney. She returned to the living room. Tobin was on his hands and knees. Moore still was by the windows. He said, "He could have been shot from that apartment across, only it was a close shot, right up against his vest."

Tobin growled, "You talk more pish."

They didn't see her.

Moore was aggrieved, "I know, Toby, but I get results, don't I, talking it out?"

"While I work."

She interrupted, "I'm going now. You'll close the door tightly when you leave?" And she added, "I'm afraid you won't find anything. Bette cleaned thoroughly yesterday."

In the elevator she recalled she'd forgotten to let Gig know about the afternoon. She would call him from the Waldorf.

3

Missy didn't like anybody at the cocktail party. Nesta was surrounding both twins. She was all over green and purple flowers, even on her tiny bonnet. Missy sat by a canapé tray and ate greedily, first the caviar, next the egg, last the watercress. Gig was out of place with his pipe and bookish hair. Jasper was bored. Nesta must have made him come; but Ann's few intimate friends, fifty and more who needed impressing most, were not bored. Not with Montefierrows and movie stars littering the place. Arthur was gurgling.

Griselda sat alone. David came over. He was smiling but his eyes were cold on her. "You can't pry Danny away from that painted doll. She seems to be an actress or something."

Griselda snorted. "She's *the* movie star, cinema, you know."

"Is that it?"

They were playing manners in front of the guests but she was trembling. His eyes hadn't moved from her and they were without meaning. She rose from the chair; David's hand was under her elbow.

"You aren't leaving. I thought we might have a bite of supper later, and a cinema."

She told him, "I'm sorry. But I promised Gig." Now to get quickly to Gig.

David said, "I am more sorry." His fingers caught hers. "You are not so stupid as you would pretend."

Missy pushed through their hands. Her mouth was oily from food and one ball of caviar teetered on her chin. David took his handkerchief and wiped it off.

She spoke sulkily, "I'm not having a good time. I'm sick and tired of this place. Let's go."

David jeered, "Because Danny makes eyes at the pretty girl."

They forgot Griselda. She inched away but she listened.

"You lie…"

"I must always remind you I am as good as Danny?"

"You are better, David, but you do not care for me. You care only for you. Danny does care for me. When he is not making a fool of himself."

Griselda zigzagged to Gig alone in the corner.

"Bored?"

He shook his pipe. "Not bored. But I'm no good at these things."

She spoke quietly. "You must wait for me. I won't stay much longer. I'd like them to leave first and I think they're about to. They want me to go with them. And I don't want to, Gig. I'm afraid if we start now they'll join us." He knew who was meant.

"I can stick it as long as you say."

She nodded, left him to join a group where she could watch the room. David spoke aside to Danny. Danny drew Nesta away for an instant. Missy's cheekbones were like garnets. But Nesta did not leave with them. She returned laughing to Arthur and his friends, and Missy's hand clutched Danny's sleeve when they departed.

Griselda gave them ten minutes before gathering Gig. The party was beginning to break. She said to Ann, "A lovely afternoon, darling. A success."

"Wasn't it nice!" Ann was in clouds.

She asked, "Have you decided what to do with Missy?"

Ann plopped to earth. "No. She's impossible, isn't she? But we can talk tomorrow, or maybe later. You're joining the twins at Morocco, aren't you?"

She wasn't. Ann's eyebrows pointed.

"Not a word about El Morocco said to me," she reported truthfully. "I'm going home. Gig's taking me."

He was waiting, vague and embarrassed in the parade of afternoon trousers.

Below the doorman asked, "Call a cab?"

She refused before Gig could speak. "We'll take the Mad. bus. It's early and a little air will help. It stops on the corner here." She wouldn't let him spend his small salary on cabs for her.

They turned from the awning. There was a Checker at the curb. The door opened and David stepped out. "We'll give you a lift."

Griselda sucked in her breath. "Never mind. We want some air." She made her voice bright and loud. Loud enough, the doorman might come out to investigate.

David said, "We've been waiting for you. We'll drop the professor." His stick touched Gig's side. "Get in."

Gig started to say something and she saw the steel. "Get in, Gig," she cried. He did. She could run for it. She stood there.

David smiled at her. "Get in."

Danny and Missy were in the back seat. They were quarreling but quietly. They didn't even look at the newcomers. Griselda squeezed in back with them. Gig and David were on the jump seats, David's cane still pointed. He tapped the window. "Twenty-one East Fifty-fifth, driver." He was polite. "We will escort you there, Dr. Gigland."

Gig began, "But Griselda doesn't want to go with you. She asked me…"

David's smile was sweet. "We won't keep her long. A small errand."

She was icy.

Missy shrilled suddenly, "If you don't leave those god-damned women alone, I'll kill you." She struck at Danny's face.

He took both of her hands in one of his and looked at her for a second. "You won't kill me," he said. He had an ugly smile. With his free hand a fist, he clubbed her on the temple. Then he turned his back on her and stared out the window. She began to sob soundlessly.

Gig was having trouble breathing.

Griselda whimpered, "Open the window, David. I've got to have air." She gulped it.

David's voice was hard. "Danny and Missy are not always the pleasantest of company. I apologize." Then he spoke to them in a language not even familiar. Danny turned forward again but he didn't speak to Missy. She hushed her whimpering but the lump on her temple would be blue.

The brakes squealed on Fifty-fifth. David pointed, "Here." He opened the door and stepped out. "Here you are, Professor." The cane was pointing.

Gig pleaded, "Griselda and I have an engagement this evening. I suggest that she join you some other time."

Danny's voice was ugly. "I suggest you get out while you can. We've been patient with you too damn long."

David warned, "Dan…"

The taximan must hear. Maybe he was used to scenes. Maybe he was afraid.

She said, "Go on, Gig. If I'm not back by morning, call Tobin."

David laughed, standing there in the frosty night. "Just a small errand. We'll deliver her back to you in an hour, safe and sound." He walked to the apartment with Gig. She wanted to scream out. She couldn't see them now and she held her breath.

Missy said, "A match, Danny?"

"Don't smoke now," he told her. She put her case away without a word.

David was back again. He couldn't have done anything to Gig in that time. He directed, "The Biltmore." They followed Missy and Danny through the revolving door, down the lighted promenade, out into the evening again.

Griselda asked then, "Where are we going?"

"A little errand." He held her arm. Missy and Danny were also arm in arm but they were laughing. They led. Their steps were quicker. Then they were out of sight.

She questioned, "Where?"

He laughed at her. "You should stop bothering your head, Griselda. We know what we are doing."

She shivered. She spoke from deep inside her, past the surface things. "I'm afraid for Missy. She is my sister."

He was sober. "She is happy. She isn't like you and Ann."

The Madison National Bank was great and gray on the corner. He turned her into the darkness, a side entrance she'd never seen. She held back. Forty-second and Madison was lighted; buses were passing and cars and there were always people. Yet no one had noticed them turn. It was as if they were invisible standing there, David holding the door for her. He said, "Come in." Her feet moved without her will and she was inside looking out into the incredible reality of street lights and street scenes.

He said, "Come," and she answered in a dream, "I didn't know banks were left unlocked."

He laughed softly, "Danny and Missy left it open for us."

She turned towards the street again and he touched her arm. "This way." He moved through the semi-dark into blackness. He walked as easily as if his eyes held torches. She was uncertainty beside him.

"What are we doing here?" Automatically she had used a whisper.

His voice was conversational although subdued. "We're going to the vaults."

She felt stairs, could see nothing. He walked as by daylight, assisting her. She was helpless. "Why are we here? We shouldn't be here. If we were caught..."

"We are never caught." It was a simple statement.

They were at the foot of the stairs. There was a needle eye of green light ahead in the corridor. At first nothing but the light was in their eyes, then Missy and Danny were behind it.

She whispered, "Aren't you afraid to show any light?"

He patted her arm. "Don't be nervous, Griselda. That can't be seen." She could see the outline of his face. Then she saw what he had seen while he spoke, something dark, taller than a carpet on the floor. Something that didn't move.

4

For that moment the silence was as the dark.

Griselda knew she was shivering but she wasn't cold.

Her teeth were chattering as if it were winter here instead of the sultry heat of the under corridor.

David's words came, cold as her throat. "Who did that?"

Missy defended. "He had to. The man saw us." David was ice. "I told you not to. It wasn't necessary." He would have left Griselda but she clung to him as he walked toward that black shadow. He warned, "Don't get blood on your shoes. Be careful where you step."

Her giggle was the sob. "I can't see…"

His fingers tightened on her arm. "Quiet."

It was just a man, not much different from Mr. Grain, only the mustache wasn't waxed. She looked away.

Danny rasped, "There's no sense wasting time. There might be another. The vault's here." He had a key. He opened the heavy door, swung it into darkness.

David said to her, "This way. Watch where you walk." He circled her past that dark blob.

Within the darkness was without feeling. Then the green flare dazzled her. Missy held it, a thin pencil with light in the tip.

Danny ordered, "The number of your deposit box, Griselda."

She was too frightened not to remember. "61117."

"I hope that is correct." His voice was without feeling. The same key was in the box that had opened the door. It opened the box.

She asked in a sudden annoyance, "Why are you opening my box? Why?"

David said, "Surely you know." He continued, "You visited your box yesterday. We want the blue marble."

If she started laughing, she wouldn't be able to stop. She bit her lip. "It isn't here. I could have told you that." She bit her lip until it hurt. But she mustn't start laughing. A man dead on the corridor floor because they didn't ask.

David opened the box. His fingers touched everything. Rubber-banded letters from Con, dated six years ago. Dated three years ago, last will and testament. She froze but he didn't open it. The box of keepsakes, prying through them, but the marble wasn't there. He didn't open last will and testament; didn't even see the letter in fresh ink, "To Con, In Case of My Death." The sheaf of bonds. Her father's watch.

He said, "It isn't here."

Missy's little voice was pointed as a sharpened stick. "Why do you waste time? Why don't you make her give it to you?"

"I don't have it. I don't know anything about it." She was husky, frightened.

Missy coaxed, "She's lying. You know she has it. Make her give it over."

Griselda caught David's arm in panic. "I don't have it. I don't!"

He said, "That's enough, Missy."

She was scornful and disappointed. She muttered, "Because she has a face."

Danny put the box back. It clanged in the silence. "Let's get out of here." He locked the door after them. Missy darkened her torch. They skirted the body there in the tiny flare. At the steps Griselda pushed close against David. Even with him beside her, she didn't like those two following in the black.

It was uncanny. They went out of the door as they had come in. Danny locked it. They walked up to Fifth; David hailed a cab, said, "The St. Regis." He added, "You'll have a drink, Griselda."

She was drained. She said, "I only want to go home. Please."

Danny was suddenly kind. "Don't worry. No one can testify against us." Then he said, "No one has ever testified against us."

David spoke to the driver. "Stop a moment in the middle of the block." He helped her out of the cab. "Shall I…"

She shivered away from him. "I'll go in alone. Please." If she began to weep now, would the taximan know? Would he help? She didn't dare. "Alone, please."

"As you will. Goodnight."

She hurried to the walk. Mechanically she watched the cab drive away. She let herself into the foyer, rang for the elevator. It gave the faint clang that meant it was waiting on first.

VI

When she pushed back the heavy iron inner cage and stepped into the elevator, she knew why David had not insisted on coming with her. It must have been the reason. Gig was crumpled on the floor. He didn't move.

Fury clawed her. The lethargy of fear, of shock, was gone. This was how David had been rid so soon of him. Another killing—nothing to the horrible twins. The elevator stopped at four. She touched Gig's hand. It was warm—too warm for death? She didn't know. He did not seem to breathe.

She opened the cage, the heavy door, held it with her knee and took his hand. She tugged at him but he was immovable, a solid lump. Someone was behind her, had opened her door. The hair on her scalp pricked. She couldn't turn; she still held that helpless hand, clutched it now.

A man's voice, a nice lazy voice, asked, "What are you doing? What on earth…"

She dropped the hand and whirled. Con standing there! Con, tall and bony, with his nice horsy face and wise gray eyes.

"Con, oh, Con!" She ran into his arms and she hid her face close to him. "Con—Con—Con…" Repeating the word over and again as if it were a talisman, her fingers like hooks on his shoulders.

His voice, still easy, "What's the matter, sweet? Boy friend passed out on you?"

She remembered. She remembered too much, that she didn't belong in Con's arms, her nose smelling his tweed coat, but above all she remembered Gig lying there dead or dying. She pushed away. "We've got to get him out of there. Help me, Con."

She held back the heavy grill again and he dragged the lump over into the narrow hallway. He dusted off his hands as if he had been hauling ashes. "Now what?"

She told him, "We'd better get him into his apartment, in bed."

Con looked down at the mound. "But where? Who?"

Her eyes were sharp at him, puzzled.

"Who is it?"

She cried out, "Con! Gig, of course!"

He looked again, then at her. His voice had lost some of the gaiety. "That isn't Gig."

"Then who is it?"

"I've never laid eyes on him before."

She stood there, realized she was tearing at her skirt. She whispered, "But he said—he calls himself Gig..." She couldn't make sense.

Con said, "He mustn't see me. We'd better get him into Gig's apartment. Does he have a key?"

"He lives there."

She couldn't move; couldn't touch him again. Con went into the shapeless pockets; found the key.

"Is he dead?" She had to know.

"Don't think so. More like a coma." He put his hand against the man's vest. "Heart's going. Not very right. Wonder where Gig is. Open the door." He handed the key to her. He half-dragged, half-carried Gig—it was Gig to her—inside.

"The bedroom—do you think?" He answered himself. "I can't figure in this. You'd hardly drag him that far. Couch is better. Have to get a doctor for him. Sure he isn't drunk?"

She shook her head. "He isn't. Someone—hurt him." She wondered if it were the gas. There didn't seem to be blood.

Con took her hand. "Come on, baby. We'll go across and you call for help. I'll hide out when he comes. Can't let the guy pass out—even if he isn't Gig."

They closed the door and went across to the other apartment. She said, "Be sure it's locked," when he closed the door. Her hands were wobbling as if she were old. She just made the couch, slowly, carefully. She clenched her fingers. She couldn't do anything now, like fainting or hysterics. Not before Con.

He followed her over and squinted down at her. "You seem pretty rocky yourself, Griselda. This guy mean something to you?"

She shook her head. "Not that. You—you…" She caught her breath. "I need a drink. A hard one." You—you'd be rocky too if you'd seen… But she mustn't talk about it; she might go under. She mustn't involve Con in this. Danny would kill him, too. And Danny would kill her if she talked.

He walked to the kitchen. She closed her eyes, just for one moment, one tiny moment. If she could only stay close to Con she wouldn't be frightened. She didn't want to die. She wanted to stay with Con. That was silly. They were divorced. Con was satisfied even if she weren't. He didn't want a baby doll wife. He'd said so before the divorce. "I can't keep up a baby doll. Excess baggage to me." Maybe she was a baby doll then. Maybe he was just trying to hurt her as she used to try to hurt him. But he was content without her.

He brought her a glass of Bourbon with ice and some water. "Better take it slowly. You're in a state. You can tell me after you drink a little."

She took a swallow, then set it down. "A doctor. We must get a doctor for Gig. Whom shall I call?"

He went with her to the phone in the bedroom. "Moriarty's my man. But you can't—he'd know it wasn't Gig…"

"I don't know New York doctors any more."

"Whom does Ann have?"

So many. One for eyes and one for heart and one for childbirth and one for children's care. But she remembered a name. Slezak. She dialed.

The servant said that Dr. Slezak made no night calls.

"Then the name of some doctor who does. It's terribly important and I don't know. I'm just a visitor here."

There was finally a name. Dr. Kane. Again she dialed, and after a space reached him. New York doctors were not as in smaller places, leaping out at every call. She tried to explain, urged, "Will you come?" until he agreed. "Ring my apartment. He isn't conscious—or wasn't..." She replaced the phone, rested her head for a moment against the head board of the bed. Then she stood.

Con caught her when she tottered. "Easy," he said. "You do need a drink—or something."

They returned to the living room. She sat stiffly on the couch. He pulled a chair for himself in front of her, looked into her eyes. "I suppose this is all a part of the blue marble."

Her eyes shivered but she nodded. "It is. Con, put the chain on the front door and see if the back one's still tight."

He obeyed, returning, asked, "Why the ramparts?"

"People have had a strange habit of barging in here without invitation. I thought it safer." She tried to be casual.

"Mm."

She asked, "Why are you here? I thought—"

He grinned. "I'm not here—officially. I had a fellow fly me up. Have to be back by tomorrow afternoon. No one's to know I've been here, baby."

"I won't tell." So much she mustn't tell. If only she could keep it straight. But this much she would remember. No one to know about Con. "Why did you come?"

He grinned again. "More than one reason. Maybe to see how you were doing. No time to go into it now. Is the marble safe?"

She whispered, "Yes," and she shivered and looked beyond him at doors but none was opening. She leaned to him, "Why don't you give it back? Why do you want to keep it? If you only knew..." She jumped at the buzzer's sound.

He nodded to her to answer. Hesitantly she went to the communicating phone. "Yes?" Then relief, "Yes, Dr. Kane. The elevator is self-running. Button four." She hung up, pushed the opening bell.

He said, "I'll get out of the way until he goes."

She held her hands tight at her side because she couldn't let him go. "You'll come back?"

He laughed. "Your eyes are like saucers, angel. I won't be out of earshot."

She heard the elevator and opened the door into the hall. Dr. Kane's mustache was to disguise his young mouth, his sobriety, his young emotions. She said, "I am Griselda Satterlee. I called you. Professor Gigland is in his apartment." Con had left the opposite door on the catch. She preceded the doctor.

Gig was limp on the couch. She caught her breath, whispered, "Is he dead?"

"No." He worked over him a long time but Gig lay there, unresponsive. The doctor's face puckered. "I've tried restoratives. I've tried everything. But nothing happens. It's like an anaesthetic but that seems impossible. He mustn't be left alone. Can you stay?"

She couldn't. "I scarcely know him. I couldn't stay here." She tried to explain just enough, that she had found him in the elevator. This wasn't Inspector Tobin but better to get the story set now. If Gig, this Gig, died, she would be questioned. The very young doctor would be questioned.

He decided. "I'll call a nurse for tonight. In the morning with Dr. Slezak..." He took the phone.

She was on edge. "Need I wait? I'd like to get to bed. I'm so tired."

"Of course." His whole face apologized. "Sorry to keep you so long, Mrs. Satterlee." He hesitated. "You don't look well. You're nervous. Would you take a sedative if I gave it to you?"

She said no. Again she crossed to her own apartment, let herself in. She didn't know where Con had gone. She sank on the couch, took up her drink. The back door was opening. Her throat was too dry to scream.

It was Con re-entering and she began to weep without sounds. She heard him chain the door. He came over to her and there was surprise on his chin.

"Don't start that angel," he said mildly. "We haven't much time and I want you to talk." He took her glass from her, went to the kitchen and returned with a fresh one for each. "I'd put you to bed but I'm afraid you'd pass out on me soon as you touched a pillow and I've got to know first what has you in such a frazzle." He looked at his wrist. "It's ten-thirty. I have to be out of here by midnight."

She had wanted him so, listening to his voice over the radio; she had thought that if only he were there, everything would be all right. If he'd only hold her hand as Gig—or whoever he was—did. But he was Con, sprawling back in his easy chair, one knee hooked over the arm. He was here, but the dreadful game must go on; he must be protected, not she; she couldn't pass the burden to him. For that would be surrender and he didn't want that. She couldn't reach one finger out to him lest he think she was trying to get him back.

She asked: "Do you know the Montefierrow twins?"

"Good God! Have you met up with them?" He drank.

She wanted to laugh and cry at his ignorance but she held her mouth taut. "Yes."

"Good God!" he repeated. He drank again. "They're here?"

She nodded.

"I haven't seen a paper—except the *Tinted* headlines." He said, "I didn't think they'd stick around here if they came. I thought they'd follow me. Believe me, I'd never have asked you to use the apartment if I'd thought you'd run into them. That's fact, Griselda." He meant it. He asked suddenly, "Anything on them?"

She answered no. She hoped he wouldn't think it was irrelevancy. "Mr. Grain, your superintendent, committed suicide." She couldn't mention tonight, not until it was in the papers. "They want the very blue marble. They say it belongs to them. Missy is with them."

"The kid sister."

"She's grown up."

He remembered. "She saw the marble once. That's how they've traced it to me."

"Why don't you give it to them?"

He spoke easily, "I don't have it."

She began to shiver. "Con—please…"

He patted her knee. "Listen, baby, I don't want that marble for myself. You ought to know that. If I did, I'd have done something about it a long time ago. I wouldn't have to be wearing my voice out plugging a border fracas now. I'd be Warbucks himself—or lying in a ditch with buzzard feathers in my hair."

She sat very still, too still. "It is valuable then."

He whistled. "Valuable!" and looked at her curiously. "You don't know anything about it?"

How could I?"

"I don't know." He laughed. "Only everyone seems to know. It's been an underground yarn for years. I never quite believed it until the blue marble came to me."

"Send it back," she urged.

Again he hesitated. "I can't. The guy who—sent it to me—got his. A knife in the..."

He was going to say a word but he didn't. She said, "Through his navel."

He eyed her, startled now. "Yeah. How did you know?"

"I don't know. I didn't say that. I didn't—"

"Uh, huh." He was looking at her panic, halfway through his eyes. Once he loved her. Once he couldn't keep his hands away from her. Now he sat there looking at her as if she were a stranger. "Sure not," he said.

Her lip quivered and she covered it with her fist. "There must be someone you could give it to."

"Believe me, honey," he was serious now, "I'd give it away in a minute if that's all there was to it. But it isn't. I'm keeping it out of sight for a purpose—"

Her eyelids tilted.

"I haven't time to spin much of a yarn," he said, "and you're better off if you don't know too much.

But the secret service is trying to round up—certain killers..."

Breath hissed in her nostrils.

His eyes narrowed. "A bunch that kill for the sport of it—or because they have to, maybe—but they kill, and they take what they want. Unfortunately they've wanted too many state secrets and sold them to the wrong parties. There's been no proof to pin on them. But they want the blue marble now." He shrugged. "If they don't get it, maybe they'll show their hands."

She didn't stir. "You say, 'they.' You know who. The secret service knows?"

"Yeah. The Montefierrow twins—and a yellow-haired doll that runs with them."

Chill was in her again.

He said, "They've put a punk on me. Irish his name is, Irish

Galvatti. Hasn't the foggiest what it's all about, except to keep me in sight. That's why I was certain, they'd handle me themselves, not hang around New York." He reassured her eyes. "Irish doesn't bother me. I keep him drunk most of the time. He doesn't move without orders. But he's a killer too. I wonder about this fake Gig."

"He isn't one of them." She was sure of that. "They've threatened him. And tonight..."

"They did it?"

"David did. He must have."

He drank. "You've got to play-act now, Griselda. Don't let any of them guess you know anything."

If he only knew.

"Don't let this Gig suspect."

"Oh, no." She wondered though.

"I've got to get on my Gig's trail. If they killed him—I'll have the hunt started secretly." He looked at his watch. "I might see Barjon."

"Are you working with Barjon Garth?" The fabulous head of the new X Division in Washington. The president's right hand man. The greatest man-hunter the country had ever known.

He drawled, "In away."

"Is that why you're on the border?"

"No. I'm there for N.B.C. But I'm not wasting time." He looked at his watch again. "I think I'll take off and make that Washington stop." He stood on his feet and she stood in front of him, steadying herself with her legs pressed against the couch.

"You're not in any danger, Griselda?"

"No. Oh, no." If he thought she were he might come back into this horror. Not because it was she; he'd do it for any defenseless person.

He hesitated. "If I thought you were, I'd do something despite my situation. I'd do it anyway only my hands are sort of tied. You see, I'm taking orders from the X these days." He repeated, "The less you know the better, but this much: I've known Garth for some time—interviews and what not. When he learned that I held two aces, the marble, and my relationship—previous relationship—with Missy Cameron, he asked me to help out. I have to let him run the game, you understand."

She did. She could even smile, lie. "Don't worry about me. I'm all right. They don't want me."

"Good girl." He went to the back door; she followed him like a squaw. "Better get to bed, babe, before you pass out on the floor." He patted her head, let his hand rest a moment there, then jerked it away. "So long."

"Con…" But there was nothing more to say, nothing she could say.

He unchained the door, turned the bolts, and went out into that horrible dark passageway. She didn't watch him disappear. She rebolted, rechained the door, tore away her clothes, and cowered in bed. She left the lights in both rooms burning.

VII

SHE HADN'T slept at all, or she had slept for a thousand years, when the banging began. Then someone was calling, "Miss Satterlee, ma'am, Miss Satterlee. It's me. It's Bette, ma'am." She opened her eyes slowly as if she were in a strange world. "It's me. It's Bette."

"All right, Bette," she called. She turned off the bedroom lights, switched off one living room lamp as she went to the door. Bette had it open on the chain. The maid wasn't alone. There was Tobin's face over her head.

Griselda closed the door, unchained it, opened it again. She didn't care. At least Tobin was safety. She could listen to him even if she were too tired to talk. Moore was there too. He took off his cap and Tobin said, "Good-morning, Miss Satterlee. Sorry to bother you again so early."

Bette explained, "They were at the door, Miss. I couldn't get in with my key."

She smiled faintly. "No, I put chains on. I feel safer, being here alone." She moved to the couch and pulled off that floor light. The two glasses, hers and Con's, she handed to Bette wordlessly. She didn't explain either action. She sat on the couch. Moore went over to the window again, opened it and leaned out, looking at nothing. Inspector Tobin sat in the chair where Con had been.

He said, "Guess you wonder why we're bothering you again."

She didn't answer. Words took more energy than she possessed.

"You see, the doc isn't so sure it was suicide."

She let her eyebrows speak.

"No, not so sure. Seems Grain was knifed before he was shot. And there would have been a lot of blood somewhere. Wherever it happened." He waited for her to say something but she didn't. "He was shot down there, but he was already dead, carried down there dead, whoever put the knife in him..."

Moore called over. "A thin knife it was. Maybe a stiletto—or a rapier. The bullet was to cover up the marks. But a way inside their paths didn't go the same way. The doc says he'd have bled like a stuck pig where it happened."

She knew what they were doing. Piling on horrors to make her talk. They didn't know that violence could arouse no emotion in her. There was none left. She stated, "They know all that?" added, "by medical examination?"

Tobin said, "Yeah," just the way Con had said it last night.

Bette brought the breakfast tray, asked, "Shall I start in the bed-room?" Griselda nodded assent.

Tobin looked at his thumb-nail. "You sure you didn't see Grain Friday?"

She was put together more compactly now. She could smile. "You don't think I knifed him?"

He pushed his hat back. "No, we don't. But maybe it happened in here."

She looked at the rugs. They didn't know about the small one. Not unless Bette had told them. Had they questioned Bette? She was careful. "I told you the truth. I dined at my sister's. After I came home, friends dropped in. I told you who. If he'd been killed here wouldn't there have been blood?"

Tobin said, "Quarts of it."

Moore nodded. "That's what we're telling you. We were wonder-ing if maybe we could take the rugs down to the lab—for testing."

She could smile. "I suppose you could. They're Con's not mine. Would it take long? A place is so barren without rugs. That small one," she pointed to it, better tell them, "was cleaned Saturday. One of the boys spilled a drink on it, and it stained. He had it cleaned."

"You know where?"

"I don't." She called, "Bette. Do you remember what cleaner returned the rug?"

The woman brought in her unsurprised face. "No, Miss Satterlee. A messenger brought the things. There wasn't any tag."

Would they notice the plural? They would. They noticed everything.

The doorbell rang. She was rigid. No one spoke. Bette and the carpet sweeper opened the door. It was Gig walking in, shyly, hesitantly.

"Gig!" Griselda clattered her cup and crossed to him. "You're all right?" She took his arms, held him off to look at

He was sheepish. "Yes, I am. I couldn't understand why that nurse was there with me when I woke up. She says I'd been out all night." He didn't notice the others until then.

Griselda drew him over to the couch. "Dr. Gigland, Inspector Tobin, Sergeant Moore. They are investigating Mr. Grain's death, Gig. They don't think it was suicide."

Gig blinked, "No? But what?"

Tobin remembered. "You were here that night. Friday night. Notice anything peculiar?"

Griselda went for a cup for Gig. If they could but tell how peculiar it was. But they couldn't. Not now.

His mild voice was saying, "I don't remember anything very strange." He was sweet. She didn't care why he was masquerading. He was sweet and normal.

There was no reason why one street noise should rise above the others through the open window. But it did. A newsboy's shout,

"Extra! Extra! Man dead in Madison National Bank—" The room was silent.

The cup and saucer slid from her fingers, crashed. She looked down at the splinters, said simply, "Oh."

Bette rushed in. "What a shame! I'll get it, Miss."

Griselda said, "Oh," again, and stood motionless.

Tobin was in the bedroom without asking, dialing headquarters. Griselda went back to the couch. Her voice sounded queer to her own ears when he returned. "What?"

"The Madison National watchman murdered. That's your brother-in-law's bank, isn't it?"

She answered, "Arthur is a vice-president."

"Nothing missing—so far as they know—haven't checked much yet of course. Didn't discover it till nine. It's in my district. We'll come back another time, Miss Satterlee." He and Moore were gone before he finished speaking.

She sank. Gig asked so quietly Bette could not hear, "You knew about this?"

She nodded tiredly. She pushed at her hair. "Oh, Lord, Gig. I'm supposed to lunch and dress Nesta today. And I can't. I just can't. Call for me. Tell her anything." She closed her eyes, didn't think while he was in at the phone.

When he returned, he said, "She isn't in, hasn't been in since yesterday."

"Did she leave a message?"

"No. I left word for her to call, that you couldn't make it."

"Thank you." She smiled up at him and he smiled back.

He said, "Poor Griselda. Better go back to bed. I'll look in on you later."

She returned to the bedroom.

"Bette, would you be an angel and stay here while I sleep? Guard the door. Don't let anyone or anything disturb me."

Bette would. Griselda removed the phone from its cradle. She climbed back into bed and she slept.

2

It was three o'clock when she woke; not enough sleep but better. Bette was in the living room, nodding over the paper.

Griselda said, "Thank you." She put a folded bill in the woman's hand. "Now go have a party. Did anyone come?"

"No-one. Thank you, Miss. But there's two wires there, Miss, that came."

She took them. Both were signed David. The first was that he had phoned to no avail and he wished to see her, would she meet him for dinner, for cocktails? The second was a follow-up. She crumpled them into the basket.

She waited for Bette to leave, chained herself in, showered. She remembered to replace the phone while she was dressing. It rang but she ignored it, ignored the insistent continuance. Dressed, she dialed Academy 9-6254, asked for Mrs. Stepney.

Ann's voice was querulous. "Where have you been, Griselda? I've called and called. Have you heard about Arthur?"

Panic filled her again. "What about him?" she cried.

"The Bank. Poor Kerrigan murdered in cold blood."

Griselda said, "But Arthur…"

"He's simply overwhelmed," Ann spoke pathetically. "All of us are. I've been flat on my back all day."

Griselda made a face at the receiver. Then she listened.

"And Arthur's been trying to get you all day. The police want to see you."

She whispered, "The police? Me?" They couldn't! They couldn't! And yet see what they had known from poor Grain's body.

"Yes." Ann went on and on. "They've been checking and nothing seems to have been touched except your deposit box. They wonder if anything is missing."

Griselda's relief was shattering. Her voice sounded too loud. "How strange, Ann! I want to hear all about it. May I come up?"

"If you only would," Ann sighed. "I need some solace. I'll call Arthur that you are on the way. There's no reason for you to go down to that hideous bank. The police can just talk to you here."

Griselda agreed and discontinued the conversation. The phone rang again while she took her black satin bag and gloves, touched her lips redder, threw her black furs about her. She could face Tobin now. At least she looked normal.

Still ignoring the phone she opened the door, thankful for the empty hallway. Opening the elevator was a hurdle but she leapt it, was grateful for its emptiness, and again for no one in the downstairs foyer. She walked to Madison, hailed an uptown cab, gave the address. Only then was she safe for the moment from the twins.

Ann was on her scarlet and cream chaise longue, languorously lovely in cream lace. Her hand manipulated an enormous chiffon square of scarlet, damp with eau de cologne. She cried, "Griselda! Never have I had such a day! Never! Are you going dancing later?"

Griselda laid off her furs and bonnet. "No. I just dressed for moral support. I was feeling wretched."

"It's horrible. But you don't know. And after divine yesterday— the cocktail party really was amusing, don't you think? And afterwards we had dinner at Morocco with those adorable twins."

Griselda's eyes were wide. She was thoughtful. "Did they return to the party?" She explained, "They left before Gig and I, you know."

Ann nodded. "We met them there at nine."

Nine. They went from the bank.

"They had the most delightful dinner ordered. A special champagne."

To food and wine.

Ann's eyes were animated. "And how they can dance. I've never been able to rhumba before, but with David!" She laughed, a woman adored, remembering.

To flirtation, to music and laughter. And a man died for nothing.

"Missy, of course, behaved abominably. Griselda, you wouldn't believe! Eating like a little pig and glowering at everyone except Jasper Coldwater. He and that Nesta were there, too, I forgot to mention and she simply leaning all over Danny and Arthur, too, though I must say David saw through her. And then Missy simply sprawled on Jasper."

Griselda jumped a little as Olga opened the door.

"Mr. Stepney is here, Mrs. Stepney, and another gentleman—a man." The second girl in her precise uniform didn't seem quite certain of the other man. "They asked for you and Miss Satterlee."

Ann said, "Yes, Olga." She smoothed her hair, painted her lips darker, and used a large, cerise, frothy powder puff. She laid away the cream lace hostess gown for one of pale green brocade, silver sandals. She poured eau de cologne on a cream chiffon square, examined her face again, and said, "Let's go in, Griselda."

Griselda didn't glance at the mirror. She followed.

It was Tobin with Arthur. Olga had a right to be puzzled, but his hat was off in this living room and he looked presentable. Arthur introduced. Ann smiled, held out her hand, gracious as if it were a social call. Griselda's smile was less real than Ann's but she could say, gaily enough, "We meet again, Inspector."

Arthur spoke. "I've asked for drinks. Tobin just reminded me in the cab that we were classmates at Princeton."

Tobin nodded. "I remember wearing blond curls and pink satin in a Triangle chorus while Mr. Stepney sang a masculine lead."

It was all charming, before-dinner chat. Tobin in the yellow quilted chair, Olga passing Scotch and soda, but Moore was probably behind that screen, under that sofa, remembering every word, every nuance.

Ann was languid. "You'll pardon my introducing shop, Inspector, but I'm simply weary to know. What have you found out about that poor man?"

He answered her but he wasn't talking to her. Griselda's nails teethed into her hand. He said, "We've found out quite a bit, thanks to your husband's"—Arthur looked conceitedly modest—"splendid co-operation. We've spent the day with our equipment in that lower corridor." He broke off to smoke. "It is amazing, Mrs. Stepney, although a cliché, what modern science can discover. For instance, there were no fingerprints, no tangible evidence of anyone having entered the bank. By that I mean what you might term 'clues.' Nothing left behind. Yet Jim Ellison, Dr. Ellison, director of our criminological laboratories, has told us that at least one man and two women were in the bank last night. Perhaps two men. His guess would be two but findings indicate positively only one. Dr. Dawes, our medical examiner, has told us that Kerrigan was killed by some sharp, pointed weapon which was immediately withdrawn. Ellison has also found that there was no forcible entry into the bank. The front door was opened by a key, as was the vault, and as was Miss Satterlee's box." He turned to her at the last words but he wasn't looking at her; he was studying her. She allowed surprise and interest to mask her face. "Would you know why anyone should search your safety box?"

She said no. She tried to reach him beyond words. "Unless they thought there was something there which wasn't there." She didn't know if she succeeded.

Olga said, "You are wanted on the telephone, Miss Satterlee."

Her fingers closed on the arms of the chair. It wouldn't do to have the maid take the message, not what the message might be. She closed her eyes, recalled swiftly Tobin's watchfulness. She went to the foyer phone.

David's voice, "Griselda, I've been trying to reach you all day."

"Really?" She must be careful what she said.

"Didn't you get the messages?"

"Yes. Just before I went out. But I was busy tonight." Tobin was coming into the foyer. He opened the coat closet beside the phone table, fumbled in his overcoat pocket. The door masked him from the living room.

David had gone on talking. "It is important that I see you."

Tobin must believe it a light friend on the wire. She made her voice trivial. "I can't tonight. I haven't a moment."

Tobin mouthed, "Hold it."

She didn't hear what David was saying.

Tobin was repeating without sound, "Hold it."

She said, "Just a moment, please."

Ann and Arthur couldn't possibly hear. He spoke softly. "If that's a Montefierrow make an appointment for later." It was a command. His eyes held hers. He was the law; obey him.

She mouthed in return, "Where?"

"A public place." He found his cigarettes, returned to the living room.

She said into the phone, "Sorry, David. You were saying?"

He repeated, "I want to see you tonight. It is important."

She hesitated, "It would have to be quite late."

"That doesn't matter."

She decided, "Eleven o'clock. Morocco."

Now he hesitated. "I wanted to talk. There's so many interruptions there."

She spoke pointedly, "I'd ask you up but the same is true of my place. Monday night usually isn't very exciting anywhere."

He agreed, "Morocco at eleven."

It seemed the safest place. The Montefierrows were known there. The photographers caught them there. Nothing could happen.

Ann's eyes were velvet. "Was that David?"

She nodded.

Her sister's voice was limp, like the cream chiffon in her fingers. "Why didn't you ask him to come up?"

When Ann was velvet and cream there was danger. Griselda was a little sick. Ann couldn't really be interested in David. She stammered, "I didn't think of it."

Ann said nothing. She talked to Tobin about the marvelous detective work of the New York police.

Olga said, "Dinner is served."

Arthur was hearty again. "I asked Toby to join us, Ann." He apologized proudly, "You can tell the day I've had, that I forgot to mention it before now."

3

In the cab going down Park, Tobin asked, "Why did you drop those dishes this morning?"

Griselda didn't know what to say. "Why—I—I don't know— I've been nervous lately…"

He stated, "And that extra made you more nervous."

Held by a red light at Sixty-fifth Street, he asked, "It wouldn't have anything to do with a blue marble, would it?"

Her eyes widened until they stung. She asked him, "What blue marble?"

He was looking out the window and at Fifty-ninth he answered, "You're mixed up in a dangerous game, Miss Cameron or Mrs. Satterlee or whatever you call yourself."

She said, "You may call me Griselda. You're a friend of Con's."

He grinned for an instant. "O.K., Griselda. I don't know if you know how dangerous it is or not. I have an idea that you have an inkling. But if you're smart, you'll get out fast."

She said simply, under her breath, "If I could, I would," but she was afraid as she said it. She added, "It's not going to do me any good turning up with you."

He pulled an old silver watch from his pocket. "We're getting there early. You couldn't help yourself. I insisted on bringing you down from Stepney's."

She repeated, "It still isn't going to do me much good."

It was ten before the hour. They sat against the zigzag blue of a wall under a shiny ice palm tree. There weren't many at the tables. The orchestra was meandering through a waltz.

The second hand touched eleven as David came in the doorway, immaculate in white tie. Attendants bowed in his direction. The maître d'hôtel beamed. David saw her but his eyes didn't change. He came through the narrow apertures to her. Tobin was on his feet.

"I must run, Griselda. The force is being kept pretty busy these days, you understand. Goodnight." He turned, "Goodnight, Montefierrow."

David bowed. He sat down, ordered drinks.

"Why did you insist on seeing me?"

He put his hands neatly on the table. "We're going to the hills for a little rest, until this bank affair quiets. Danny was foolish there."

She didn't say it but murder wasn't foolish, it was insane. She didn't want to speak of insanity before him. Because of course he was that, both of them, and Missy too.

He said, "We thought you'd find it more comfortable to join us."

She cried, "Oh, no!" Be shut up with them for a week—no!

His mouth curved. "In view of the fact that the police are so interested in your activities—"

She shook her head decisively, "I wouldn't want to." And she said with deliberation, "I'll enjoy a breathing spell."

"Perhaps." He smiled at her with his lips. "Dance?"

She shook her head. She looked at his eyes. "Why did you do that to Gig?"

He actually laughed. "Oh, Griselda! My dear Griselda! You hold that against me?"

She was furious. "Of course I do. He's a friend of mine. To find him like that."

"You found him? That was unfortunate."

It was amazing, frightening, how he could express feeling with hands and mouth and voice, and never a change in those still black eyes.

She demanded, "Why did you do it?" and he answered, "I was afraid he might attempt to follow us, interfere with our plans."

"But why?"

He smiled again. "Because of you. He is in love with you."

She felt her cheeks warm. "That's absurd."

"Not at all. I might be in love with you myself."

She looked away. "You couldn't be in love with anyone."

"That happens to be true." He spoke softly, chilly. "But if I could, I might be with you. You are exceptionally lovely, even beautiful. The way your hair shines, the storm of your eyes, the molding of your body…"

She knew she looked a fool. She was embarrassed.

"Danny and I are too sensitive to beauty. It is sad." He tapped one of his own cigarettes, did not offer one to her. "Were it not so we could end this more quickly. And end it we must eventually. You understand?"

She did and was iced again.

"We will have the very blue marble."

She stated flatly, "I haven't it."

He didn't look at her. "Perhaps eventually you will find it for us."

She thought before she spoke. "Don't you think if I could give it to you I would have long ago? Don't you think I'd do anything to get you out of my life?"

"Almost anything." He smiled. He beckoned to a waiter hovering nearby. "Could you fix for me a little favorite? Say—brook trout boned, en casserole with pecans and filberts, and warmed with perhaps a sour white wine? I need something of exquisite food. My brother and I and our party are going up to the country for a week. A place called Canaan in the Berkshire country. Perhaps you know? A lake near where we will fish and lead a simple life." He laughed. "But before simplicity I must have my fill of luxury. Hence—" He spread his hands.

"I personally will inform the chef," replied the man, and he went across the tiny waxen floor towards the kitchens.

Griselda said, "I shouldn't think you'd be giving away your hideout."

He shook his head. "You do not understand. This shall be in the papers. John always gives news to the reporters. Tobin will not think we ran away. If he wishes us, we are there. Meantime nothing will be discovered of the bank mishap, and something else will take its place. Then we return."

She spoke, anger surging in her again. "It isn't as easy as that to have murders forgotten."

He was deliberately patronizing. "It is obvious that you are lacking in experience, dear Griselda."

She hated him. She was surprised at herself, the venom she put into her words. "They know there were two women and at least one man in the bank last night."

He accepted that information thoughtfully. "And what else?"

"They know that Grain was stabbed before he was shot. They think it happened in my apartment. Tobin and Moore woke me this morning. They were about to take the rugs for examination. I don't know what else. When we heard the extra cried…" Tears, not sudden, she'd been fighting them for too long, were in her eyes.

He said, "I don't pity you, Griselda. If you would give us the marble—"

Only two words could express herself to him. She said them bluntly. "Shut up." He did.

Silence, strained silence, was better than talking with him. There was something even better. She started to rise. "I'm going home."

His fingers touched her wrist. "Sit down." He was looking towards the entrance. She raised her eyes. Missy was there, Missy in white satin fringed from the waist in shining crystal leaves, nothing above the waist but a wisp, a strap, crystal leaves wreathing her pale lemon hair. Little murmurs zigzagged about the room. Jasper Coldwater was tall behind her.

Griselda wondered aloud where Danny was, guessed silently. There was a groove between David's eyebrows. He said, "She's drunk. She's not allowed to drink. That damn cinema cretin."

Griselda said quietly, "My wrist is practically broken."

He was grieved. His profusion of apology was more embarrassing than his compliments had been. This was sincere. "I forgot."

She was grateful that she was not Missy.

He said, "I must get her home before she is too much the fool. You will forgive me, Griselda. If you will but wait…"

She looked at him, then away. She couldn't understand the fury bottled in him but it was ugly. "I'll finish the dish, David, then go."

He nodded as if not hearing her, made his way to that table. She watched. She couldn't hear what he said but Missy was swaying as she stood and the color was out of her face. Griselda didn't watch them leave. She ate and she gulped in unknown fear when someone shadowed her chair. It was merely Jasper.

She urged, "Do join me. Taste this."

He was plaintive. "That twin took your sister home. He didn't like her being out with me." He couldn't understand. Even husbands were delighted to have their wives out with Coldwater.

Griselda asked, "What did he say to her?"

"I couldn't understand it. It wasn't English. It didn't sound like French or anything I've heard." He protested, "She called me."

She told him, "I wouldn't worry about it. They're all so foreign."

He was eating from David's plate. "Um." He touched his lips with the napkin. "This is good. Where's Nesta?"

Her eyes were wide. "I haven't seen her. I called."

He was a little annoyed. "She hasn't been back to the hotel since Sunday."

She wouldn't let fear touch this. Not Nesta. Too obvious where she was with a new man in tow. She laughed, "She'll turn up when she's bored."

He agreed. "I don't doubt it." His voice was complaining. "But it is hard to go on making excuses to Oppy. He keeps calling me, as if I should know."

"Tell him she's gone fishing." She had finished to the last drop of sauce. "I'm going home now."

He said, "I'll drop you. I'm tired of this place.

I'm tired of New York. I want to go back to Hollywood. But I have to see Nesta off to London. We're a romance. Damn Nesta. Damn the pictures. She's sailing next Monday—if she remembers."

He summoned the cab. Griselda said, "I wouldn't worry about her. She won't forget her public and the Korda picture."

"She makes me sick." He saw her to the elevator, opened it for her and she was spared that. Going up in it she began to laugh. The Montefierrows had done one thing. They even made movie stars seem normal.

VIII

No one in the hallway. For once, no one in her apartment. She searched, all lights blazing, before removing her coat, before putting down her bag. She chained the front entrance, re-examined the back one. She considered calling Gig but discarded the idea. It was too good to be alone. She undressed, showered, put on pajamas with green tadpoles cavorting in pattern, tied back her hair with an old pink ribbon and daubed an icy cream on her face.

It had been so long since she was alone; she had forgotten how good it was. To be able to think. Think a little on Con, but that hurt, wanting him, after four years she should be over that want. She'd thought it was gone, at least leashed, but she knew now it would never be finished. Not think of Con. At least he was safe on the border job, or would be if he'd stop the midnight flights. He was safe. Anyone was safe away from the Montefierrow twins.

Tobin was nice. At least he'd be nice to know if he weren't pecking at you, if he were a friend. But why did he want her to meet David? Sergeant Moore was nice too. But they were watching, waiting to close in. What would they do to her? She hadn't killed—but she'd known and not told. They could do something to you for that. Even if you couldn't tell, with nothing to tell at first, and after, after afraid to speak. Afraid, not exactly of death but of something unknown, something more horrible than death. And afraid always for Con. She wouldn't mind what the police did to her; they could shut her up, take her life. She wouldn't like it but she wouldn't be frightened of them. Tobin said it was a dangerous game, more dangerous than she knew. It was more dangerous than he knew. But there was still time. The twins wouldn't really hurt her until they had the very blue marble. If the X-men would only hurry, if Con only realized how they must speed.

And where did Gig fit in? If he weren't Gig, who was he, and what did he want? One thing certain, he wasn't a killer. But what was he doing here?

Too many circles. Missy. Missy ought to be saved. She was too young. Ann, jealous because David had called her sister. What was David doing to Ann? David couldn't feel. Didn't Ann know that or did he pretend to her?

Nesta. Jasper. But they were normal. Again she smiled at considering Hollywoodies normal.

No more thoughts. Sleep. That was best. She relaxed, snapped off the bed lamp, and closed her eyes.

The dream woke her, dreaming someone was in the room, but that couldn't be. She stirred without opening her eyes, relaxed again. But there was someone in the room, someone watching her in the dark. She didn't want to open her eyes but her arm reached to the light.

"Don't turn it on."

Missy's voice. Griselda sat upright in bed. The room wasn't dark. There were reflections from street lights below. She could see Missy's outline perched on the far window ledge like an organ grinder's monkey.

She had closed the Venetian blinds earlier, although the windows were left open. Missy must have raised that one. Perhaps that noise had wakened her.

She asked, "How did you get in here?"

"Through the bathroom skylight."

She was small enough. She looked like a little boy in the half light, a dark cap on her head, dark knickerbockers and shirt, even long dark stockings, boys' oxfords. She was smoking one of her little cigarettes.

Griselda could see the flame in the tip, brighten, dull, brighten, dull, nervous smoking. With her bare toes she loosened the bedclothes, if she had to get up in a hurry—

She asked, "Why did you come here?"

Missy spoke simply as a child. "I'm looking for Danny."

She was amused. "And you thought he'd be here?"

Missy said, "If he had been here, I would have killed you."

Griselda prickled. Her small sister meant that. She told her, "I haven't seen Danny since Sunday." That horrible night. "Why should you think he was here?"

Missy repeated, "If he were here I'd kill you."

Griselda spoke sharply, "You shouldn't talk that way!"

The youngster snapped back at her. "Why shouldn't I? He's mine. I won't let anyone else have him." She added slower now, "David's mine, too. I won't let anyone have him."

Griselda prickled again. She wished to explain but Missy added, "I don't have to worry about David. He doesn't want anyone."

Griselda breathed again.

"I don't suppose you know where Danny is?" Missy asked the question with rare politeness.

"I haven't a notion." That wasn't quite true. She went on, "I thought you were all going away."

Missy said bluntly, "Not until we get the blue marble."

"I mean," Griselda explained, "for a—breathing spell. David said…"

Missy gave a big sigh. "If David says we are, we are. But he can't make Danny go if Danny isn't here."

She was losing her fear of this gamin. She lighted a cigarette, was curious. "Does David know you're here?"

The child tittered. "He's asleep. I put some drops in his night cap." Suddenly she was angry. "The way he treats me!" Her voice was sly. "But he's not as smart as he thinks. He won't wake up till I want him to." Then angry again, "I don't care if Danny beats me. He doesn't mean it. He only does it when he's mad. But David doesn't get mad. He's like a god."

Missy wasn't rational. What had made her this way? They had, of course. But how? Drugs? Subconscious hypnotism? Griselda shivered. She spoke as to a child. "I don't see why you stay with them. It can't be much fun being beaten."

The younger was defiant at once. "I don't have to stay. I stay because I want to. And not you nor anyone can stop me."

"I wouldn't try." Griselda spoke softly.

Missy dropped her cigarette out of the window. "I'm going now."

"Yes. You should get some rest if you're going to the Berkshires in the morning."

"Rest?" She laughed noisily. "I'm looking for Danny." She started towards the bath.

Griselda said, "You can use the door."

Missy spoke sullenly. "I'll go as I came." She went in darkness.

Griselda waited long enough before she struck a match and looked at her watch. It was just four o'clock. She didn't think she'd get much sleep before pounding on the door would wake her again. She was correct. Nine o'clock. The inevitable Tobin. With him Moore and three other men in plain clothes with hand boxes.

Tobin said, "Always sorry to disturb your rest, Griselda, but orders is orders. The Commissioner doesn't hold to sleeping in the mornings. We want to make some tests. We have a warrant if you're interested."

"I'm not." She smiled. "You go ahead." There seemed to be spring in the air through the opened bedroom window. The breathing spell had begun. A good day to look into Gig. But she wouldn't use this phone. Dressed, she opened the door between.

The men were working swiftly, silently, with electrical gadgets. One would measure, speak code-like figures, another write. "It looks fascinating."

Tobin said, "This takes time. But we'll leave you ship-shape."

In the elevator she was startled by an idea. Bette must know Gig was not Gig. She had said nothing. Was she in on this too?

The air did have spring in it. It was good to taste. She went to Fifth, walked down to Saks and used a phone booth. She dialed Columbia University, asked to be connected with Dr. Gigland. A connection was made and another girl's voice spoke. "Dr. Gigland's office."

"May I speak to him, please?"

"He's just gone over to his class. He teaches the next two hours. Could he call you?"

She said no and added, "I will call him again."

Nothing to do until noon. Easy to while away time in the shops. But she was curious. Or rather she wanted to know, to be certain. She called the St. Regis. "Miss Cameron or Mr. Montefierrow."

The clerk was cordial. "They left this morning for the country. They will return in about a week. Is there any message?"

She said no, hung up, breathed easily. She could enjoy a week of her vacation. She shopped until noon.

This time she was connected with Gig.

"Griselda?" It was his voice.

She told him, "Those beastly twins are out of town. I feel celebraty. May I come up to the campus and lunch with you?"

He laughed. "There isn't a place with anything fit to eat up here. I'll come downtown. I have no more classes until tonight."

There seemed no reason to press the campus. He was there. He was Professor Gigland. At least you phoned and asked for Dr. Gigland and were given this Gig. The greatest university couldn't be in on a misrepresentation.

He said, "Let's make it the Plaza. If you're really celebrating. About half an hour."

She demurred. "I asked myself. It's too expensive."

"I can afford to take a girl to a nice lunch once in a while." He was firm, gay. "Professors' salaries aren't that poor."

2

She met him in the front lobby. There were hyacinths in the window boxes outside the great comfortable dining room. And the park trees were hinting at greenery. He asked her, "Why did they go?"

She had to take time to answer, studying the menu. "For a rest, David said. They've gone up to the Berkshire country, Canaan, he said, fishing. But it seems early for that." She selected eggs, creamed with crab, melba toast, coffee, and an ice. "At any rate they're gone for a little and I feel reprieved. I'm so tired of having them turn up at the apartment at any hour. Even when they aren't there I'm afraid to go to bed at nights lest I find them under my pillow."

He laughed.

She said, "Let's talk about you. Do you realize I don't know anything about you except that you're a friend of Con's?"

He smiled now. "I know more about you. Con talks plenty of you."

She flushed, was warmly happy inside, then realized it wasn't true. Con didn't know this man. She raised her lashes. "Nice things, I hope."

He nodded. "Naturally. Although in Con's offhand way."

He sounded as if he knew Con intimately.

She put her lips straight. "We aren't talking of you but of me. No fair evading. Tell me about yourself. Have you taught at Columbia long?"

"I've taught ever since I finished college."

"Persian art?"

"Sounds dry as dust, doesn't it?" he smiled. "But it actually isn't. Art and archaeology." They were served. He buttered a piece of Vienna bread. "I've been doing a little research and learned something about"—he put the bread in his mouth—"the blue marble."

Her eyes widened. "It is Persian?"

He shook his head. "The earliest written account of it is Renaissance although it is believed that there is somewhere a manuscript dating back to the Comneni that tells of it. Alexius certainly knew of it for both Hugh of Vermandois and men with Walter the Penniless sent back word of it. It may have come to Alexius' attention with the Petchenegs or Seljuks. It is certainly Eastern. There are some who believe that Marco Polo was the first of the Western world to view it." He broke off to ask, "Have you ever seen it?"

She laughed. "I? I never heard of it until all this started." She gestured briefly.

He said, "The Italian manuscript describes it. But the marble itself only turned up recently, about the mid-eighteenth century in Egypt."

He took a forkful. "I've taught all morning. I'm starved." He drank from his coffee cup. "According to this paper, the marble is small, smaller even than a typical marble, and of a perfect sky blue. It was the author of the manuscript who called it the 'so blue marble.' It is unblemished, yet there is a way in which it can be opened. How, he didn't say."

She ate to cover thought. It couldn't be opened. There was no opening.

"Within it is lined with gold. Engraved on either side is a map." He ate rapidly, continued: "Of course there's a bloody trail wound about it, years of violence, theft, torture, murder—"

She asked, "But what is the map of? Why is it so valuable?"

He wiped his mouth with his napkin. "The map, according to the manuscript, tells where to find a secret cache wherein are stored the riches of the world. The author describes rubies big as the moon, cut diamonds and emeralds, moonstones, pearls—like pebbles on the ground. Gold, of course, mercury, platinum…" He sighed. "The usual Arabian Nights tale. But also," he leaned across the table, "there is supposed to be something of real value there. Hieroglyphs telling the secrets of the greatest lost civilization, of the day when the sun was harnessed, as we would like to harness it, when gravitation was controlled as we haven't dreamed of controlling it. When there was Utopia on earth." He smiled. "Of course no one but the twins with their strange minds would believe that part of the fairy tale."

She was serious. "If it were true, I should think it would benefit man to have the cache discovered."

"Unless the wrong person discovered it. You wouldn't care to have the twins dictators of the world."

Her eyes were frightened. "No!"

"Naturally enough wrong 'uns have always been after it, men wanting gold more than benefit to civilization. No decent person has ever had a chance. But then, no one has ever been able to keep his life and the marble."

She shivered in her marrow.

"Not even for long enough to use the marble."

She said, "I should think anyone who got hold of it could make a copy of the map."

He smiled. "That's been tried. But it's no good. Death steps in."

She wondered why these secrets were hidden away.

He said, "There's a legend of barbaric hordes threatening, corruption eating away the people, good turning into evil, the great ruler deciding to lock away these things of good and of beauty until there should again arise those who could use them wisely. The secret he encased in the very blue marble. It, too, he hid away. And it disappeared. The obvious is that there hasn't arisen anyone worthy of employing the secret of the blue marble. If there had, bloodshed wouldn't still be staining it."

"Yes."

He lighted her cigarette. "The legend of the blue marble has come down the centuries by word of mouth in every country."

She interrupted, "The strangest part of all is that it should turn up in New York. Or at least be traced here. The twins insist they traced it here."

"To you?"

Was he after it? Was that what this was leading to? But he was mild as ever behind his glasses, curiosity alone there.

She told him, "Not exactly. They say Con had it."

He laughed.

She joined in. "Silly, isn't it, but they insist that he had it. And the fact that Con's allowing me to stay in his apartment seems to make them believe I took the marble." She spoke with fervor. "It may have been a legend of the years but I never heard of it in my life until I met those two." She tossed her head. "To tell you the truth, research or no research, I still don't believe in it."

"If it isn't real, how do you explain the twins' determination, the murders—Grain…"

She said, "For that matter I don't explain Grain. Why should they have killed him unless they thought he had it?"

Gig told her, "Grain evidently interrupted them while they

were searching your apartment. Perhaps saw them go in and went to investigate. So they killed him. The bank guard…"

She spoke quietly, "You know they did it."

"It was the same way. Those damn sword canes."

"I was there." She watched the tablecloth, traced her forefinger. "I don't dare give witness. They would kill me as carelessly."

"Yes."

"But it doesn't mean to me there need be a marble. They are obviously not sane. Those persons without balance usually do fix on an hallucination, don't they?"

3

He paid the check and they went out again into the sunshine. They crossed Fifth, walking lazily down to the Fifties.

"It's coming closer to me. When I'm arrested I don't know what I'll tell the police."

"The truth."

"Somehow I don't dare. It's queer. I've always thought that innocent persons who became involved with criminals were absolutely idiotic not to go to the police first thing instead of muddling along, getting in worse stews. But here I am. Afraid—of what I don't know." But she did know. Unless she stayed with them, fought her way through, Con would return. And the twins would kill Con. She had to keep him away. She looked at Gig.

"It makes me furious when I think why. Why? Because two utter strangers want a mythical blue marble which I don't have." She laughed a little. "It's crazy. You know it is."

He admitted it was, put that way. They reached the apartment. She said, "Come in with me."

Tobin and his men had gone. The living room was pin neat. She tossed off her hat, put on her pale horn-rims.

"You can gather how brains run in our family. Missy, the henchman of murderers. Ann…" But she wouldn't expose Ann. "Myself, about to be arrested."

He was soothing. "You're all right. You needn't worry. Ann is sane, although she seems a bit social-minded. Missy…" He tried to comfort. "She's young. Maybe you can get her away from them." The telephone was ringing. "Shall I answer?"

"I'll get it."

It was Ann, inevitably, "Where have you been, Griselda? I've been trying for hours—"

"I went out to lunch."

Ann said, "Won't you come up? I need company. I'm terribly low. Stay for dinner. Arthur will probably be out—he's head and shoulders in this bank business."

She agreed to come. "It's three, in about an hour." She hung up; the phone re-rang.

"This is Jasper, Griselda. Have you had any news from Nesta?"

She told him no.

"I must find her. Oppy is furious. He wants publicity. He says he isn't paying a small fortune for our Waldorf suites to have us enjoy ourselves. We've got to do something, Griselda. Oppy is threatening to fly East tonight if she doesn't call him. You know how awful he'll be if he flies—"

She didn't quite see how she herself figured in it. But Jasper was a querulous child. She said, "I have a hunch she's gone to Canaan, Jasper."

"Where's that? I never heard of that."

"It's upstate, about one hundred and fifty miles, two hundred, something like that. Stall Oppy for tonight and we'll call her there."

He wailed, "I've been stalling and stalling, Griselda. He won't take any more."

"Tell him the truth. No, wait—wire him now that you'll call him at midnight, Eastern time. I'll come down to the hotel after dinner—I'm going to my sister's—and we'll call Canaan, talk to Nesta. Then I'll do the talking to Oppy."

He was jubilant. "You will? That's wonderful, Griselda. You're wonderful." He rang off.

She sighed out loud. Jasper was a perfect infant where his producer was concerned. But then all the O.C.H. stars were that way about Oppy. When she returned to the living room, Gig said, "I'll be running along. Looks as if you've a pretty heavy schedule."

She grimaced. "And I came East for a rest."

When he had gone, she hurried. Get out of here before anyone else called. The phone was ringing as she left the apartment. She took a cab; her ankle dress at this hour wasn't for buses.

4

Ann was on her back on the one twin bed, waggling her legs in the air. She let them fall with a soft thud. "All dressed up again! Who is it tonight? David?"

Griselda smoothed her hair. "No. I have to see Jasper later."

Ann swung her legs aloft again. "I've been so low. And I feel a little heady, like maybe a cold coming. So I decided I might as well stay in and do a little waist-lining. Join me?" She looked like a little girl, on her back, her hair tumbled, white silk shorts on her hips.

"Your waist line's perfect, angel." Griselda spread out on the chaise longue.

"You are popular," Ann told the ceiling, counting one-two one-two between sentences. "David last night, Jasper tonight. And you don't even exercise. Maybe that's my trouble. Just an athletic girl." Ann didn't sound low. She was gayer than she'd been in years.

Griselda was comfortable. "Maybe it is. As a matter of fact I think I'm the one who needs exercise or something. No one ever calls on me save for business."

"Morocco and David! Business?"

"It was, believe it or not."

"Did you have fun? He dances so excitingly."

She didn't want Ann to think on David. She said bluntly, "It wasn't fun. Missy came in drunk and David took her home. Jasper took me home."

"Was Jasper with you?"

"No. With Missy."

Ann let her legs down, thump, turned on her stomach. "Isn't she revolting, Griselda? Of course she always was." She pushed herself up and down in some fashion on her forearms. "This is grand for the stomach. You should try it. But then you don't have a stomach. Babies make stomachs. Little wretches. I don't see anything we can do for Missy."

"Nor I." Griselda corkscrewed backwards to put out her cigarette.

"Where are you and Jasper going? Dancing?"

"Lord, no!" She laughed out loud. "Jasper wouldn't take me to a shooting gallery. I'm small fry. I told you it was business."

Ann was on her side now, scissoring one leg, then the other. "You certainly aren't designing frocks for Jasper!"

She laughed again. "Ann, how silly! No. Oppensterner, O.C.H.'s big boss, is having a fit because Nesta isn't around getting publicity. I'm the soothing syrup for Oppy, or I'm going to try to be."

"What's the matter with Nesta?"

"Off with Danny no doubt. She hasn't been around since the night of your cocktail party."

Ann sat up on her knees and looked in her dressing table mirror. "She was with us at Versailles after the party. But she did leave with Danny."

Griselda yawned. "Well, she hasn't been seen since. That's Nesta all over. Give her a new man and she's off the face of this globe until she's bored. The only trouble is that this time Oppy's paying out his precious dollars to smear the Coldwater-Fahney romance all over the front pages and he does like value received. Also she's to sail the first of the week to make a picture with Korda, and Jasper's afraid she won't even remember that." She yawned again. "Why I have to act as wet nurse to Oppy's stars, I can't see. But I'm dragged in on it. I seem to be dragged in on everything these days."

Ann jumped over the foot of the bed. "Well, it is exciting! Movie stars and European playboys and police inspectors—I feel like a schoolgirl again." She opened her clothes closet. "I'm going to dress up too. Maybe I can make Arthur take me out. We could join you and Jasper."

"It wouldn't amuse you." Griselda rested her head. "Just telephoning. First Canaan, then Hollywood."

"Why Canaan?"

"If my hunch is right, that's where Danny and Nesta are romancing."

Ann began to carol, "Ro-mance, Ro-mance, you came in the early dawn—or words to that effect. I shall wear my red crepe with the golden stars. If Arthur doesn't want to go out maybe I can get David to take me."

Griselda stared. If Ann hadn't heard from David, why was she so gay? She stated soberly, "David's in Canaan."

Ann swung to her, her eyes narrowed. "David? Not here? What do you mean?"

Griselda nodded. "I thought you knew. He and Missy, and supposedly Danny, went this morning."

Her sister's mouth was tight. "It can't be true. I had a note, and flowers, masses of golden orchids, after I talked with you." She took the note from her jewel box.

Griselda read, "You will see me soon," and a scrawl of letters spelling the signature. She put it down. "He told me last night they were going. I called this morning, to make certain."

Ann didn't say anything. She was dressing but the fun had gone out of it. Words crowded Griselda's mouth but she couldn't speak them. If she could only tell Ann, warn her. But a little would be discounted as jealousy; all, she didn't dare.

Ann was brushing her smooth dark hair. She was nasty because Griselda knew about David. "Why do the police keep after you?"

Griselda answered out of her own annoyance. "The superintendent's murder."

"But I thought he committed suicide." Twenty smooth strokes.

Griselda began to giggle. "I thought it was heart failure." She couldn't stop laughing. She stuffed her handkerchief across her mouth but she couldn't.

Ann turned from the mirror. "Griselda! You frighten me."

She was quiet then. Mustn't frighten Ann. Mustn't let life touch Ann. She wiped her eyes, trying to stay quiet.

Ann returned to brushing. "Besides I don't see what that man's death has to do with you."

She spoke quietly. But she didn't want to talk about it. She might laugh again, laugh instead of crying. "It happened in my apartment." Quickly she remembered. Even Tobin didn't know that. She added, "At least that's what the police seem to think."

Ann wasn't that stupid. She was glancing sidelong at her, thoughts crowding out of her eyes. Griselda knew her first remark had gonged with fact; her second was a swath of hasty dust which hadn't blinded even Ann's eyes.

IX

Jasper was taste embellished with elegance. White pajamas of such heavy satin they hung like velvet, black rough wool lounging coat lined in rosy fur. His black curly hair was brushed to sheen. There were Russian boots of soft white kidskin on his feet. But this wasn't to allure his guest. He had to maintain his glamour to the hotel servitors, more, he had had nothing to do since eight o'clock but make himself beautiful.

He greeted Griselda as crossly as if she were a member of his family. His face was petulant. "Where have you been? I've been shut up here all evening waiting for you. I thought you'd forgotten."

She laid off her own coat. "I couldn't get away." Still annoyed with Ann, she said, "Some people find it dull with the Montefierrows out of town."

Jasper stated, "I loathe all the Montefierrows."

And I, she amened silently. "I want a nice drink, Jasper, a nice heavy one. And quickly. And a cigarette." She threw off her hat, put on her glasses and sank in a chair. He began work at the rolling bar.

He said, "If you don't make Nesta come back, Oppy is coming East. He'll be loathsome. I didn't want to make this trip anyway. Romance with Nesta! She positively revolts me. I don't see how anyone can romance with her. I don't even see how that loathsome blond Montefierrow can. It shows just how revolting he is."

She ignored him, reading his evening *World-Telegram.* The Madison Bank tragedy was buried now, but there was an editorial.

He came over, "Taste this."

She did. "It's good. Let me have four swallows and I'll call Canaan. And stop worrying about Oppy. I'll handle him." Anyone with a little intelligence could handle Oppy. The producer hadn't any; Jasper had less.

He took a neat one. "You act as if you don't know how loathsome Oppy can behave."

She went on reading the paper until she was relaxed. "Have the tabs sent up, Jasper." She moved over to the phone, asked for long distance. "I wish to speak to the operator at Canaan, New York."

He complained, "I can't have the tabs sent while you're on the phone."

She laughed. "I'm not used to the luxury of a hotel. I forgot. We'll get them later," and, "Canaan operator? I wonder if you could connect me with some friends who have just gone up to Canaan from the city. The name is Montefierrow."

The name meant nothing to the girl in Canaan.

Griselda tried again. "There would be three or four in the party. Two young men, one blond, one dark, twins. A very young girl, pale blonde, and perhaps another woman."

The description struck. The operator said, "I know the party. They're in the Wilson place. But they don't have a phone yet, Miss."

She hadn't dreamed of that. She sighed, "But they are in Canaan?"

"Yes, Miss. They're here."

She said, "Thank you. Make the charge to Jasper Coldwater at the Waldorf-Astoria." She had forgotten what that name could do. The voice at the other end crackled with excitement.

She hung up, said, "Get the papers now."

"What did you find out? Is Nesta there?"

She drank. "Get the papers. I'll tell you."

He called the desk. "Send a *Mirror* and *News* to me. Jasper Coldwater." His voice was honey-sweet but his face was annoyed. She talked on top of his words. "They're up there. But they've no phone."

He was upset all over again. "No phone? What are we going to do?"

She begged, "Calm down. We could wire. But Nesta certainly isn't using her own name. She never does on tour. And it doesn't seem as if the twins are. The operator didn't know the name. There are the papers." He walked towards the door.

He was listening to her but when he opened the door he was the great Coldwater, a treat to the bellhop. He closed it again.

"There's your damn papers." He tossed them to her, was patient, "Do you know what we're going to do?"

"Yes, darling, I do." She was opening the pages. "And you can't imagine how I'm enjoying this little excursion into normality." She was. She was as comfortable as if her shoes were off and her face in cream. But wouldn't the fans howl! Go to Jasper Coldwater's rooms for a normal existence. She grinned at him. "Don't look like that, Jappy. Fix me another drink while I tell you."

He obeyed, still disturbed, irritated.

"I'll take care of Oppy tonight. I promise you. Get us a little spare time. Tomorrow you and I will go to Canaan and bring Nesta home. How's that?"

He liked it. He beamed, not any of his silly screen smiles but a real grin, a silly one. "You're a genius." He handed her the drink. "That will do it. She'll have to come back if we go for her."

"Right." She turned the pages. "For a movie star you're less interested in publicity than any I've ever met." She tossed over a section. "There's your picture with Missy at Morocco last night, and a lot of blah. Also you will notice that the Montefierrow twins have gone to the Berkshires for a respite and some more blah."

He smoothed his hair. "It isn't bad of me—for a news flash. She's a funny little brat. Is she really your sister?"

"I don't believe it but she is."

"She called me and asked me to take her out last night, see and be seen, she said. Then she let that fellow run her home like a scared rabbit."

She spoke under her breath, "Maybe she was." Aloud she said, "I'm going to call Oppy now. No use sitting around until twelve." Again she asked for long distance. "I want to speak to Jules Oppensterner, Beverly Hills, California, reverse charges." She gave the necessary data. "There may be a little trouble reaching him, if you'll call back..." She hung up, went back to the papers.

It didn't take ten minutes for the call to go through. Oppy's excited voice not waiting for a greeting, "Jappy, is this Jappy?"

"This is Griselda Satterlee, Oppy."

"You don't say. I expected Jappy to call. About Nesta. Where is Nesta?"

Griselda spoke calmly, "Now listen, Oppy, be patient. Nesta is where Nesta often is."

"Patient! Now is no time to be patient!" He was beginning to scream. "Nesta shouldn't be there now! I'm paying big money to have Nesta with Jappy in the Waldorf-Astoria. Where is she?"

Griselda said, "Nesta is in Canaan. In the Berkshires."

He screamed, "What good does that do? Nesta in a Berkshire!"

She answered briskly, "It doesn't do you a bit of good, Oppy. Now stop yelling and listen to me."

Jasper's eyes shone. No one who worked for Oppy dared talk that way.

Her words came fast. "We tried to reach her tonight but there's no phone. Tomorrow Jasper and I will drive up and get her. By tomorrow night we'll have her back in New York and publicity all over the papers. Do you know who she's with? Well, I'll tell you. The name wouldn't mean anything to you but he's one of the wealthiest and most famous young men on the continent, from an old New York family but he lives abroad. And he's also sailing next week. Think what he can do for Nesta in London! She's not wasting time. She's building up for more publicity than you ever thought off, world-wide publicity. Maybe it will even be a real romance..."

"Well!" came weakly from the wire.

"So if you'll only be patient, Oppy, we'll get Nesta back to catch the boat and you'll have all the front page stories you want."

She could see him, wiping his bald forehead. He went into explanations; he was patient; he understood. He was only upset because Nesta was so flighty.

She ended. "We'll have her call you tomorrow night." She hung up, began to laugh. "He eats from your hand."

Jasper said, "Not from mine. You are wonderful. No one can talk that way to Oppy."

"I can." If she could talk that way to others—but no thinking of that now. She finished the drink. "Now for tomorrow. Call Oppy's New York man, tell him to get you a car. We'll have to get up early if we're going to locate Nesta and be back here tomorrow night. Let's say we leave at nine. Now don't make faces. It's as hard on me as on you. But it'll take us at least four hours to make it up there—or near that."

"But nine o'clock—that means I'd have to be up at I don't know what hour to get the car and all." He didn't like it.

"Have the hotel take care of calling for you. Let's say nine-thirty, get in by one-thirty. We don't want them to go out on us, fishing or what."

He sighed. "Nine-thirty. It's revolting."

"It revolts me too and after all it's not my affair, getting Oppy's problem child on the boat. I don't know why I'm in on it anyway."

Jasper spoke quickly and worried. "You won't walk out on me now? You'll go along?"

"I'll go."

"I will sound my horn before your place at nine-thirty on the dot," he promised.

"No, not my place!" Tobin might not let her go. She mustn't get involved in all of that again, not tomorrow. "Meet me in front of the Plaza."

"But…"

"Do it," she ordered. She put on her silly hat. "Goodnight, Jasper."

"Goodnight. You're a peach."

For the moment she was afraid he was going to turn on the charm for her, but he didn't. He let her put on her own wrap; he didn't offer to see her home.

In the lobby below she saw Tobin. He was just sitting there; why, she didn't know. She hoped he didn't see her, hurried out the door.

2

She walked the few blocks to the apartment, decided then to spend the night out. No use risking her early morning callers; Gig would take her in. And he needn't be embarrassed tonight. He had twin beds. She rang his bell. He answered.

"It's Griselda. I'm coming up."

He was ready for bed but in the hallway waiting. "Anything wrong?" He had that scared expression.

"Nothing at all. Except I've decided to spend the night with you."

He hesitated but only slightly. "All right."

"You don't mind?" She was opening the door of her place. "No one else in there?"

He was red. "Of course not."

"Come in while I take off these things. I'll explain."

He sat in the living room. She talked towards it while she undressed, put on brown silk pajamas, her heavy white robe and slippers.

"I have to make a get-away early in the morning and I'm afraid if I stay here I'll have my usual callers. I could have stayed with Jasper if I'd thought."

"You mean that movie fellow?" He sounded shocked.

"Yes." She selected clothes for the drive, gray tweeds and matchings, a sweater golden to match her hair, tooth powder and accessories. She put the small things in a weekend case, carried the clothes over her arm. "We've located Nesta. Jasper and I are going to drive up to the country and get her. Oppy, their boss, and incidently mine in a minor sort of way—I've done some designing for his stars—at any rate, Oppy is having a catfit out in Hollywood because Nesta's not playing ball on publicity." She returned to the living room and said, "Get the lights, Gig. Besides she's sailing Monday and after all she ought to do something for her board and keep, not chase after Danny Montefierrow."

They crossed to his apartment. She hung her clothes, remarking, "We won't have to break rules tonight with two beds." He flushed and she was sorry. "I won't talk foolishly, Gig. You're grand to help me in this way."

He smiled a little, shyly, "I'd do more than this for you."

Remembering David's statement, she was herself embarrassed. She asked, "Do you have an alarm clock by any chance? I'll just leave my bag here when I go. Get it later."

He didn't. "I always wake by seven-thirty, to get to the University by nine. I like my breakfast in leisure. Shall I call you?"

"Please." She asked which bed, climbed in.

He took the other. "Did you learn the results of the investigation in your apartment?"

"No, I didn't." Her cigarettes were on the bed table. She took one; he tossed the matches to her. She drew in smoke. "I've had a fairly nice day. It is restful having the twins out of town."

He commented, "Yet you are invading their territory."

"Yes."

"Just why?"

She spoke slowly. "I don't exactly know. I get drawn into these things. I felt sorry for Jappy, he was so upset, and I think Nesta ought to come back." She couldn't, wouldn't, express her vague fears. But nothing would happen to Nesta Fahney. The twins wouldn't do anything to her. They wouldn't have any reason for that. And they wouldn't let Missy hurt her.

They'd be there to see that Missy didn't do anything. There was no reason to have any worry about it. She had finished the cigarette.

Gig put out the light. Then he said, "You mustn't do this too often, Griselda."

"What do you mean?" She didn't quite understand.

His voice was subdued. "Even professors are human."

He couldn't see her face when she answered, "And you're Con's best friend."

He didn't say anything else except goodnight.

3

Jasper *would* have a glittery car. It was enormous, black as a well-groomed horse, low-slung as modern furniture.

They drove along the smoky blue river and the little towns had the first look of spring. It was after twelve when they reached Chatham, then off the highway through rolling farmyards, to the few houses of Canaan.

The Wilson house was a nice old New England-ish place, white frame, even a cupola. It was set in a treey yard already greening. Vines on the house must be roses in summer. They climbed the steps to the porch, twisted the old-fashioned bell, heard its metallic ring.

Jasper had a new tremor. "I hope she won't be mad. Nesta's definitely revolting when she gets mad."

Griselda rang and rang to no answer. "I suppose they're out picnicking."

Jasper said, "Let me try." He was annoyed. He pounded.

She told him, "It rings."

He rattled the knob. "It's unlocked."

"Country style. We didn't think."

They went inside. It was a big cheerful house, paneled with sun, too many ferns but that was to be expected.

Griselda called, "Hello. Anyone home?"

They wandered out through the dining room and kitchen, back into the spotless parlor bedroom.

Jasper was cross. "They aren't here."

"Obviously," she answered. "Let's go up. Make sure they haven't flown the coop. It's so tidy. It doesn't look as if anyone was here. Not even an ash for diversion. They must have brought Bette along."

She led the way up the stairs; he followed. She said, "Bedrooms! We're getting warm." The first was open, again perilously clean. She was dubious at the starch in every inch of lace and linen.

"You don't suppose we've made a mistake in the house, that we're making ourselves at home in some stranger's place?" Then she saw tucked under the edge of the old marble-topped bureau something that had escaped notice. "No, we're right." She picked it up, the diversion, a gold-banded cigarette stub with the tiny gold letter. She laid it on the hand-painted blue forget-me-knots of the pin tray. He was in the hall again.

He said, "Right or wrong, I'm looking for the bathroom."

He opened a door, said, "Yes, they're here." She peered in after him. Nesta's opened bag was on the floor, clothes messily frothing out of it. She followed Jasper into the room. The door had hidden the bed. He was staring at it, the color of mayonnaise. His hand faltered towards the brass bedpost. She spoke furiously, "Don't touch anything!"

It must have happened a long time ago. It didn't look like blood; it was like ugly brown paint all over the sheet, on the flowers of the rug, all over the white net and lace that didn't cover Nesta's body. It was Nesta. Those were her rings on the hand, her silver-tipped toenails. It was her hair, what there was of it, on her shoulders. There wasn't any face at all.

X

JASPER SAID, "I'm going to be sick."

She clenched her nails on his arm. "You can't be sick. If I'm not sick you can't be sick."

He gulped. "I can't—help—that—I'm—going—to b..."

They heard the call from downstairs. "Hullo? Company? Who's there?"

Her fingers tightened on him. "Come on." She pulled him out, closed the door after them. "Come on." She dragged him to the stairs, looked down on the face of a stranger, a nice young stranger with curly yellow hair and sunburned face. He seemed as surprised as she. She ran down, still pulling Jasper with her. She demanded, "Who are you?"

He began, "I'm..."

But she looked beyond him and didn't listen. She dropped Jasper's arm; her eyes grew wider and wider; her head began to go around and around. It looked as if it were Con coming through the living room into the hall. Then her eyes went dark and she knew she was fainting.

She was lying on a bed when she remembered again. She sat up quickly but this bed was clean. She put her head down again; it was still dizzy like a merry-go-round. She had seen Jasper in the chair.

She was surprised at how tiny her voice sounded. "What has happened?"

He looked resigned. "So you've come to. I don't know what is happening. After you fainted the one called Con said Good God he didn't think he'd be so much of a shock, and I told him it wasn't him, it was Nesta dead upstairs, and that I was going to be sick and I was—loathsomely. And he and the one called Irish…"

She whimpered, "Irish?"

"Yes, Irish. Ridiculous name. They went upstairs and came racing down and told me to stay with you until they returned." He added, "I don't want to stay here. I want to get out of this revolting place. And what will Oppy say?" He closed his eyes at the mere thought.

She wondered, "What is Con doing here? And Irish?"

He was amazed. "Do you know them?"

"I know Con. I used to be married to him. I've heard of Irish."

He looked out of the window. They were in the parlor bedroom. "They're coming back. I suppose they brought the constable and he'll ask us foolish questions."

It was really Con in the doorway. "Feeling better, honey?"

"I think I can get up."

He told her, "Don't. Not yet. Wait until I come down." He went away. She closed her eyes; Jasper's were already closed.

They could hear men's steps upstairs, then coming down. Con wasn't alone now. The young blond boy was with him and a quiet farmer man.

"Don't get up, baby. This is Ed Schaffer. He's the deputy. And this is my friend, Irish Galvatti. Mr. Schaffer, my wife, Mrs. Satterlee. And if my eyes haven't deceived me, Jasper Coldwater."

Jasper admitted it.

Con sat on the edge of the bed near her. Irish leaned against the door. Schaffer squatted on the window ledge. He said, "Mis' Wilson's going to have a fit when she's seen what happened to her bedroom." He seemed in a way to relish the idea.

Con said, "Now, baby, if you can give me an idea of what happened?"

She nodded. "Jasper and I drove up from New York this morning to get Nesta." She shivered. "Nesta Fahney." He held her hand. "It was about one o'clock I think when we reached Canaan, a little after. I asked at the postoffice and the man directed me here. We thought they'd gone picnicking or something and we started looking around to make sure this was the place. When we looked in that room…" She was weak again.

Con said, "Steady."

She opened her eyes. "We'd just seen her when you called from downstairs."

Schaffer twanged, "Anything you got to say, Mr. Coldwater?"

If he said it was revolting or loathsome or the most revolting sight he'd ever seen, she would scream. He didn't. He said, "Nothing."

Con said, "You can understand what a surprise this is to us, Mr. Schaffer. Irish and I needed a rest. We rented the place by mail."

Schaffer nodded. "Yes. Mis' Strombaugh was expecting you. She cleaned the house spick and span last week. Then Sunday night these folks come for the keys, said they was friends of yours. Said their names was Mr. and Mis' Green. I didn't lay eyes on them but I expect that was the girl. I wonder where the man's gone to."

Con said, "I never met Nesta Fahney. I never saw her before except on the screen. Irish never did either. I wonder who the man was."

Griselda feared to speak but Jasper said wearily, "It was Danny Montefierrow. That's who it was. She went off with him Sunday. She didn't come back."

Con acted as if he'd never heard the name. Schaffer hadn't. Irish twitched but didn't speak.

Con patted Griselda's hand. "You didn't know I was coming back so soon, did you, baby? I've been saving it for a surprise." He explained to Schaffer. "I've been away on an assignment. I'm a radio newsman."

Schaffer said, "Sure. I've heard you speak, Mr. Satterlee."

"My wife's been in New York. I was planning to wire her and here she is."

The law wasn't dumb. "How did you happen to pick Canaan? Most city folks haven't even heard of it."

Con said, "I prepped two years at Berkshire, and I spent one summer at a camp on Queechy."

Irish wanted to say something. He gulped it. "We just come this morning, had to ground at Albany. Then we picked up that rattletrap and drove down here. I was sure surprised when I saw folks in the house." His alibi unloaded, he felt better.

Jasper opened his eyes. "Do we have to stay here? I haven't had a bit to eat since breakfast."

Schaffer yawned. "No sense starving you to death, I guess. Go on down to the hotel and get Mis' Strombaugh to fix up something for you. The Sheriff's coming up from Chatham and a coroner. We'll need you to tell us a few things so don't leave town until I say so."

Con promised, "We won't, Sheriff." He braced Griselda, "Think you can make it, kid?"

She had to hold tight to him. She didn't mind. "I'm dizzy. Probably it's no food."

They all went out. Schaffer stayed on the porch, waved. Irish languished at the black motor, "Jeez, what a boat!"

Griselda said, "We might as well all drive down together."

Jasper was still saffron. "I can't drive, Griselda. Look at my hands." They wobbled.

"Let me drive it." The yellow-hair was in at the wheel, his hands tender among the dash-board gadgets. Jasper climbed beside him. Con handed Griselda in back, sat by her.

He wasn't playing a part with her now. "How the hell did you get in this mess?"

"I told you. Nesta disappeared. Oppy—Oppensterner—was badgering Jasper. I said I knew where she was and that I'd drive up with Jap to get her." She began to shiver. "I didn't think she'd be dead. I didn't know it."

Con barked, "Don't snivel."

They all went into the old frame hotel. Con called Mrs. Strombaugh, parched, ginghamy.

"Ed Schaffer says to feed us and I think you'd better let us have a room. My wife's not feeling so well." He smiled his confidential smile. "Maybe we could have food in there?"

The woman liked Con and she couldn't get over the great Coldwater. "Well, I should say. You come right along." She took Griselda's arm.

Con turned away. "I've got to phone. You all go on with Griselda. I'll be up in a jiff."

They watched him cross to the postoffice before they followed the hotel keeper. Irish's eyes slanted dubiously. Griselda lay on an old-fashioned double bed again. Jasper sank in a chair.

Irish watched out the window. "I'd like to know who Con's calling in New York." Griselda glanced at him, but his face was untouched as a child's. "Who do you think he's calling?"

Griselda answered, "Probably the newspapers. He used to be a newspaperman. And it's a big story."

Jasper sat down again, worried. "Oppy'll die when he reads about it in the papers. Do you think we could wire him?"

Griselda said, "Let's eat first."

Con banged in, threw his hat on the bureau, and straddled a chair. "I called Toby and he's..."

Griselda stiffened. "Inspector Tobin?"

Irish started over, belligerent. "What you want to do that for?"

Con said, "Shut up. Do you think I want to be stuck up here for the next two weeks playing ball with hick sheriffs? Toby'll guarantee us and get us back to New York before Christmas."

Irish licked his mouth. "You got no right to be calling in the New York police."

Con took a bottle out of his pocket, unscrewed the cap, swallowed twice, put it back. He wiped his mouth with the knuckles of his hand. "I said for you to shut up. I covered you up on why we're in Canaan, didn't I? Suppose I'd told that guy that you had orders to rent a big dump in the country and that you were pea green because you'd get the finger put on you if you didn't get it rented? So I helped you out. Suppose I told him that?"

Irish was peaish again. "You wouldn't do that, Con."

He lit a cigarette. "Suppose I told him the truth, that the only reason I'm along is because you went across the border, without orders, and got yourself in such a mess that you couldn't get back in the States without me guaranteeing you, and that I got you back in because I have a sneaking liking for you after having you on my tail for months, and I didn't want you to be bumped off because you couldn't obey orders."

Irish muttered, "I didn't mean it, Con. Forget it." Shame was on his face.

"I'm not forgetting it." He banged the chair around. "Now suppose you tell me who sent those orders to you."

The boy's eyes rolled. "I can't. Honest to God, Con, I can't!"

He broke off to the knock, to Mrs. Strombaugh and four gangly girls, all carrying good-smelling platters, all with white pieces of paper to present to Jasper. The girls sidled to him. He was gracious. He signed, handed the papers back, then made his first statement for the public. "I just can't talk. No one will know what

Miss Fahney meant to me." He turned his back, took a maroon square from his pocket, and blew his nose. It was a good scene.

Mrs. Strombaugh was saying, "Now, if there's anything else you want, you just sing out. Couldn't do so well not being regular meal-time and no notice, but it's victuals." She looked proudly on the chicken platter, the apple pies and applesauce, the hot biscuits, piccalilli, currant jelly, green beans, coffee, cream gravy, potatoes. "Had to fry the potatoes 'stead of mashing them. Knew you didn't want to wait for no potatoes to boil."

"No, sir!" Con saw her to the door, closed it after her and the string of girls. He put his back against it, continued, "You can't tell me. Well, you can tell me this. Did you rent that house to have a place to murder Nesta Fahney?"

Jasper seated himself at the table and began to eat. Griselda joined him.

"Honest to Christ, no!" Irish was livid to his curls. "I never even heard of her. I swear to Christ!"

"Answer this one and keep your voice down or it'll all go back to Schaffer." Con interjected to the table, "Save some for us," then back to Irish, "Why were you ordered to follow me?"

Irish stared at him.

"It didn't have anything to do with a blue marble, did it?"

The boy goggled. He whimpered, "You've known all along. You've known the whole damn thing!" Rage ate at his face. Griselda cowered. Jasper looked up curiously. "You've been making a fool out of me!"

Griselda screamed, "Look out, Con! He'll kill you!" She jumped in front of Con, but he shoved her back into the chair.

"He won't kill me. I took his stinking gun away from him last night but he doesn't know it." He looked at her furiously. "And if anyone is going to kill me keep your puss out of it!"

She swallowed the throat lump and nibbled again.

Jasper said coldly, "Do you and your friend have to stage your revolting scene now, Mr. Satterlee? Why don't you eat first? It's really quite good."

Con said, "Smart idea." He swung a chair to the table, watching the boy. "Sit down, Irish, and eat."

Irish took a step. "I'm getting the hell out of here."

Con mumbled through a chicken leg, "As you will. But it won't help you much to tie up with the Montefierrows right now."

Irish licked his lips again, started to speak, then sat down and ate.

2

They heard the plane. Jasper laid down the movie magazine and came out of the chair. Griselda lifted her head. "That's Tobin." Both looked out the window. They went back to their places.

Jasper sighed. "I hope he gets things fixed up quickly. Do you suppose that Con reached Oppy? I don't think I'll go back to Hollywood until this blows over. What was that fight about at lunch?"

She closed her eyes. "I don't know."

Jasper threw the magazine aside. "Do you think we might go find them?"

She shook her head. "Con said for us to stay here, together." He was rotten to her, but he didn't want her to be alone. He'd insisted Jasper stay with her.

They waited. It was a long time before the others came; it was twilight. Con, Irish, Tobin, Schaffer, and the Sheriff of Hudson County, his name was Dardess.

She swung her legs off the bed, tried to flatten her hair.

Tobin said, "Hello, Griselda."

Her smile was weak. "You'll find me all over that room."

He nodded. "Yeah. I figured so."

Jasper didn't care about the law. "Did you reach Oppy?"

Con nodded. "Poor old goat. He was crying over the phone, after he got over the first shock. He's flying East."

Jasper turned away.

Tobin put his chair in front of Griselda. Con lounged beside her.

"Now, suppose you tell me about this. You didn't say you were coming up here."

"I didn't know, Tobin." She explained it step by step until she and Jasper were in the room; there she stopped. She couldn't say anything about Nesta.

He nodded. "Where are your pals? The twins?"

"I haven't seen them." She insisted that he believe her. She couldn't say anything about the twins either. Not with Con here. He would go after them if he knew, and they were killers. "I thought they were with Nesta."

Schaffer drawled, "They're up at Queechy Lake. We've sent word for them to come down."

Dardess was an orator. "Must have been a tramp. The way she was chopped up."

Jasper wobbled towards the bathroom. Con put his hand on Griselda's knee, hard. It helped.

"No ceevilized body'd do that," he concluded his address. "We get a sight of tramps in the spring."

Tobin asked softly, "You wouldn't know anything about it?"

She denied. "No, no! I've told you the truth." She knew who did it. Of course she knew. She wouldn't say. Not unless she could tell of the twins too. They'd made Missy what she was.

Tobin spoke dryly, "Yeah. I think you're safe about this."

Jasper returned. He was laundry white. "May we go back now?" He collapsed in his chair.

Schaffer told him, "Sorry, but you'll all have to be at the inquest in the morning."

Tobin added, "Mere formality, you understand."

Jasper walked to the door. To their questioning faces he said, "I'm not leaving. I'm just going to get a room and go to bed." He half-banged the door after him.

Dardess asked, "Suppose he means it?"

"He does." Tobin strolled to the window.

Dardess lit a cigar. "What beats me is what a movie star like Nesta Fahney was doing up here anyway!"

No one spoke. Irish stood in the corner, his fingers nervous. Con held Griselda's knee. Schaffer walked. Tobin said, "There's a big car coming in now." Schaffer and Dardess went out.

Irish bleated, "I better get me a room if we have to stay all night."

Con said, "Sit down."

Tobin turned, "It's the twins."

Griselda's throat was dry. "And—Missy?"

He nodded, went out

Irish pleaded, "You said yourself the place would be overrun with photographers and newspapermen as soon as the planes could get here."

Con said, "Hide in the bathroom if you don't want to see them. Tobin's going to bring them up here."

Irish shot in; the bolt clacked. Con and Griselda didn't say a word until the corridor door opened. David in hunter's green coat, black boots, a crop; Danny in sand color; Missy, a tiny boy in jodhpurs, checkered jacket. Three city vacationers. The three officials were behind them.

David came to Griselda. "This is horrible. Inspector Tobin just told us. I'm too shocked to be lucid."

Danny wiped his forehead. "I can't believe it. It's impossible."

Missy said, "She was so beautiful," but behind her face a leopard licked his chops.

David's dark brows raised. "And how ghastly for you, Griselda, to discover it."

She nodded, "Con, these are the Montefierrow twins I've spoken of." She completed the introductions, "My husband, Mr. Satterlee." They shook hands, everything mannerly.

Con said, "You don't remember me, Missy?"

She wriggled. "I remember your name. And the wedding."

Griselda spoke again. "I don't believe you've met my sister, Inspector Tobin, my other sister, I mean."

"Only downstairs. I've heard of you." They shook hands, Missy dimpling up at him like a child. Jasper Coldwater had a word for it: revolting.

Dardess was impatient of the preliminaries. He rolled his cigar from the left corner of his oblong mouth to the right. "You folks knew the deceased?"

It was commedia dell' arte: David, Danny, Missy, all feeling for their cigarettes, the monogrammed ones, all lighting them from separate matches.

Danny spoke first. "Know her? Yes. She drove up here with me on Sunday night I'd mentioned the place and it appealed to her. She was worn out from her Hollywood schedule and had a hard London session ahead. She really needed a rest. She asked if I'd mind if she came along."

Schaffer's voice was gentle. "Why did you claim to be husband and wife?"

"Oh, that!" Danny didn't give his schoolboy smile. He was solemn, respectful. "She didn't want to be known. She explained how in the cinema there was no privacy and she needed it. And also," he was delicate, "she didn't wish anyone to be shocked, our staying together. Although the house was large enough, as you know, for a half dozen or more. That is why." He seemed to think it was well-explained.

Danny went on, distraught now, but Griselda watched his eyes. They were like glass, as if they did not know what his voice and hands and brows were doing.

"I don't know who could have done this fiendish thing. My brother and Missy," he spoke as if she were a little girl, "drove in early Tuesday morning."

David took on now, pleasantly, easily. "We liked the idea of the lake rather than inland. Nesta—Miss Fahney—decided not to move on with us. She was to sail the first of the week for her London engagement and thought she should get back to the city although wishing to stay on here. We left early. She said she would sleep a while longer, leave in the afternoon. We thought that was what she'd done." He shrugged. "You can't imagine the horror of your news to us."

Missy was malice but no one could know. "She was so beautiful."

Danny's crop twitched.

Schaffer's easy voice came again. "What I'd like to know is how you moved into Wilson's place when it was already rented."

Danny seemed surprised at the question, genuinely surprised. "We rented it through an agent, a Mr. Galvatti."

Griselda's mouth straightened. Irish was to stand the gaff then.

"Mmm." It was Schaffer again. "Irish Galvatti?"

"Yes. That's the name."

"Where is that guy?" Dardess wanted to know.

Con said, "I sent him out to get some air. He was getting jittery."

Tobin spoke aside, "Is his alibi real, Con?"

"I'd oath it, Toby."

Danny asked, "You mean Galvatti is here?"

"He was here," Con said.

Schaffer remarked, "Even if he didn't kill her he'll have a few things to answer for when he comes back—if he does."

"He'd better come back," Con said. "He's paroled to me out of Mexico and I got to get him back in."

"Paroled for what?" Dardess demanded.

"Got mixed up in a knife scrape. But I'm telling you he couldn't have killed Nesta Fahney. He hasn't been out of my sight."

There was pounding at the door. "Probably the news hounds." Tobin opened it a crack, held it. You could hear voices. "What you doing here, Toby? What the hell, Toby!"

He said, "Sit yourselves in the lobby or the bar. We'll give you all the dope in a little while. But you can't come in here."

"Who's in there? Got the killer?"

"If you won't play ball, you get nothing."

They went away, noisy.

Griselda whispered, "I didn't hear the planes," and Con said, "I did."

Tobin came back, sat down again.

Con continued, "You say the dame's been dead for twenty-four to thirty-six hours at least. We were still West then."

Danny spoke. "We've been at the lake since early yesterday morning."

"And Griselda was in the city," Tobin told them. "I saw her at the Waldorf last night. Plenty of alibis."

Danny smiled wistfully. "What good are alibis? They can't re-create a beautiful girl."

David said, "If there's anything at all we can do to help clear this up, call on us."

"You're still planning to stay up here?" Tobin asked.

David swung his crop. "We've taken the Queechy cottage for this week. We plan to sail for home at the end of that time."

Tobin crossed his legs. "I thought you'd come to make us a longer visit."

"Sorry." David smiled. "Business brought us over, and it takes us back."

"Your business here is finished?"

"It will be by then." A charming smile.

Tobin rose. "I imagine Sheriff Dardess will want you for the inquest. That right?"

Schaffer said, "Nine in the morning."

Dardess cleared his throat. "I expect we ought to be seeing the press, eh, Inspector?"

"Yeah."

They filed out. Griselda undertoned to Con, "Don't leave me here alone."

He walked the twins and Missy to the door. "See you at dinner? Or are you back to the lake at once?"

David nodded, "We'll probably be here. Nice to meet you."

More politeness. Missy behaving as a sweet child, which she had never been. Then they were gone. Con locked the door.

He said, "Lie down again, sugar. You need it." He pushed her back on the pillows as he walked by to rattle the bathroom knob. "You can come out, punk."

The whisper came through. "Is the door locked?"

"Yeah. Come out."

Even then he didn't, not until Con said, "Well, come on. If you've been listening, and I know damn well you have, you ought to know by now that I wouldn't doublecross you."

"I'm not afraid of you." The match for his cigarette was as in wind.

"But you are afraid of certain other guys not so far off. All right. I get it. Now listen, Irish, it so happens that a bunch of us want to get back home so we'd just as soon not have any more killings around here. That's the only reason I'm getting you out of this."

"Oh, God, Con!" He was shaking. "Get me out and you can write your own ticket. You don't know—"

"My imagination's up to par, thanks. You do as I say and you'll get out whole."

Griselda was weary. "I don't see how you're going to do it."

"I do. You're going to get under that bed, Irish, and stay there until I tell you to come out."

The boy's eyes were round, like blue marbles.

"Griselda stays in bed. Downstairs there's the press. There'll be some guys I know. I can trust them. They're going to get you out of here tonight and fly you back."

Irish twittered. "I'm afraid. I'm afraid, I tell you."

Con's Jip was disgust. "How you ever got into the Montefierrow bunch, I don't know." He shouldered the boy. "You're not afraid of me. I've been square with you. I didn't tell them it was a woman you killed down there, did I?" He flung him away. "Stop being a sniveling idiot and get under that bed. It'll be dirty and hot, but it's better than the twins." Irish bolted, wiggled under. "Now, Griselda, I'm going down and have a few drinks with the boys. You get up and lock this door when I go. Leave the key in the lock. Put a chair under the knob. When I come back I'll holler and you'll know it's I. If anyone else knocks, you're asleep. And if anyone tries to break in, you yell bloody murder. Understand?"

She nodded, eyes wide. He bent over her and kissed her mouth, so quickly she didn't know it had happened until it was done. "O.K., kid."

She followed, locked the door and braced it, went back into bed. Con had kissed her. But it didn't mean anything. She knew what it was. She'd seen him kiss other women. It was commendation for being a good sport.

XI

Con didn't come back. But the twins couldn't have hurt him. Tobin was there. Besides she'd kept quiet; she hadn't ever said a word against the twins. They wouldn't hurt Con when she'd been good.

Once Irish whispered, "Could you get me a drink of water?" She did; shoved it under. She was afraid of him, too. She was afraid of everyone, everything. She didn't deserve Con's kiss.

It was dark. She turned on the light. There wasn't any lamp, only a top light. She looked to see if Irish showed but the old-fashioned white bedspread hung to the floor. Someone knocked, once, again. She held her breath. Someone went away. She tried to read the fan magazine of Jasper's. Inanities. Griselda Cameron Satterlee, rising young fashion designer, has gone to New York for a month's vacation. Nesta Fahney and Jasper Coldwater leaving on the Sky Chief. Nesta smiling. It is rumored Nesta and Jasper are two-ing, although both deny.

Footsteps, noise, knocking. Con's voice, "Wake up, Griselda! Let me in." She scurried to the door.

Con had been drinking. He was lively. "'Lo, honey babe. You guys know my wife?" One, called Tom; one, Skipper; one, Tookey; one, Quip, and Tobin. "She discovered this." A swarm towards her. Con halted it, "Not now. She's got to eat. Tobin's going to buy you dinner while we…"

Quip had a bottle, Tookey, cards. They were taking off their coats, rolling up their sleeves, settling their hats. One said, "I'll get a coupla more chairs out of our room."

Griselda took her bag, went into the bathroom. She washed her face, lipsticked, combed her hair. She came back, put on her hat and coat and her glasses, took up her gloves.

Con put his arm around her shoulder. "Hurry back, now. No tricks, Toby."

There was laughter in the confusion. Her cheeks were pink. She and Tobin went down the stairs. The dining room was crowded with others like those upstairs. There was a table saved for her and Tobin. He said, "I've eaten. There's no choice but it's good. Con thought you'd prefer an escort in this mob."

She was grateful to him. She was afraid of the twins. She mustn't be alone.

She said, although she knew she should not, "I'm sick with killings—senseless killings…"

"I should think you would be." He was kind. "Did you see Nesta killed?"

"No. Oh, no!" She began to eat hurriedly.

"Grain?"

She shook her head.

"You were at the bank. You saw that man die."

She swallowed, kept shaking her head senselessly.

He said, "We've definite proof, you know. Grain was killed in your apartment. You were in the bank that night. You were in Nesta's bedroom."

She knew how trapped things died, their hearts pounding too hard, their bones like sticks.

He leaned to her, "Why did you come to New York at this particular time? What's your tie-up with the Montefierrow twins? Why were these three murders committed?"

He was waiting for an answer. Words crammed her brain,

choked on her tongue. She broke out, "I can't tell you. I can't tell you anything. Don't you think I want to?" Tears blinded her. "If I'm put under oath I know I'll have to talk. But I won't now. I—I can't." Water spilling on the fried chicken.

He sighed, passed over a spandy handkerchief. "Mop up. I can't figure you in this, Griselda. Con thinks you're O.K. He's even introducing you as his wife to put you across to Schaffer who isn't dumb, and to Dardess who isn't smart. Maybe Con knows you better than I. He should. All I know is that whether you're innocent as you look or guilty as hell, you're in this thing up to your neck."

She touched her neck with one finger. She didn't speak.

"Did you see the hatchet?" Tobin asked.

Her throat was stuck. "What hatchet?"

"The one that cut up Nesta."

Her breath said no.

"It was in the sheet. We've sent it for prints. If there's any on it the Montefierrows weren't there. They don't leave calling cards." It came so suddenly, she jumped. "Where's the blue marble?"

Her reply was mechanical. "I don't have it. I don't know anything about it."

He escorted her to Con's room. The door wasn't locked. The five were still at the table, matches for chips, the air dusty with smoke.

Con yelled, "Join us, Toby?"

"Not you crooks. I'm off to bed."

The newsmen protested volubly.

Toby said, "Goodnight," banged the door.

Con pulled out his watch. "Nine-thirty. At nine-forty-five, Skipper, you go up and talk to him. Griselda, honey babe, you get yourself ready for bed."

She eyed him. "I didn't plan to spend the night."

He looked back at her, then his mouth was a grin. "Oh. My bag's in that closet. Help yourself."

She found pajamas, dark paisley, bluish, greenish. She undressed in the bathroom, rolled up sleeves and legs, came back to the bed and leaned on it. The men ignored her. She picked up the fan magazine but she didn't read it.

Tookey said, "Quarter to, Skipper."

"O.K." They checked over the matches, paid off to Quip, Con and Tookey. Skipper said, "Give me ten minutes, then shoot." He went out.

Con's watch lay on the table. They were more noisy now. Con locked the door. He said, "Keep it up." Tom began to sing. Quip harmonized badly.

Con reached under the bed, hauled out Irish, whispered, "Don't say a word, punk. Go in the bathroom and take off your things." Tom went with him, still singing. Tookey stood against the corridor door. Tom emerged in the yellow jersey, the gray flannels. "I look like a god-damn pervert."

Irish came after him. He had on Tom's un-pressed suit. Con pulled the hat down over the yellow hair, looked at him.

Tookey said, "Give him goggles."

"Need mine," Quip protested.

"Me, too." Tom held his.

Con spied. "Baby's!" He pulled them from her nose, put them on Irish. "O.K."

Griselda wanted to know, "What am I supposed to do?"

"You don't need them as much as I. Besides you're better-looking without them." He pushed a bottle under Irish's nose. The boy drank until he said, "Enough. You know what to do. Irish, keep your mouth shut and play ball. And may I never see your puking mug again." He pushed him doorwards.

Tookey was on one side, Quip on the other. They linked the boy's arms, took up their song again, made an epithetic loud-sounding farewell. Con yelled after them, banged the door, wiped his forehead with his hand. He went to the table, shook the last drop from the bottle into his mouth. Tom was by the window. "There they go." Faint discords in the night. A car noising away.

Tom announced, "I'll sneak out but not in these damn canary feathers. Give us your coat, Con."

"Bring it back in the morning."

"Oke." He winked at Griselda. "Pleasant dreams."

Con locked the door, spraddled a chair. "Wish I had a drink."

"You've had enough."

He looked at her as if he'd forgotten she was there. "Not by half."

She put down the magazine. "Will they get him away?"

"Those guys would cut Toby's throat for an exclusive." He began to take off his shoes. She folded, unfolded the pajama sleeves. He took off his shirt, scratched his back. It was like five years ago. "God, I need a drink. You don't have any?"

She waved her head.

He opened the closet door, kicked out his bag, rummaged for a toothbrush, shaving tackle. He left the bag a cuckoo's nest. He always had. He went into the bathroom. She sat on the outside of the bed, her hands folded.

When he came back he said, "You'll have to spend the night with me. Those country cops think we're married. They needed a respectable touch what with movie stars and international soc boys."

He put out the light. His cigarette was a tiny rose madder circle. She wriggled to the far side of the bed. His side creaked when he swung in.

"We're all washed up." The circlet was cerise, then rose again. "But if you don't keep to your own quarters, I might forget you're you."

Her voice was so tiny he might not have heard it. "I wouldn't mind."

XII

THE CAR was whirlwind. Con on the wheel, Tobin by him; Griselda and Jasper held tight to the back tassels. You couldn't hear what
the two in front were saying.

Jasper wasn't saying anything. Griselda was choked with words
but silent. The coroner's verdict, "Death at hands of person or persons unknown." Unofficially, "Probably a tramp." Oppy chrome
green from his air trip with bulbous tears wetting his face. David and Danny and Missy, their precise answers, polite, amazed,
their helplessness, and their unshakable alibis. They said they were
returning to New York, first to the lake and then New York. Tobin and Con decided to drive, not fly. Tobin was afraid of something. Con was afraid too. He wasn't afraid for her. They were all
washed up. He'd said so. She didn't want ever to leave him again.
She adored him, the back of his head, with the hat shoved there.
Her fingers bit into her hands. Maybe he'd keep her on awhile. A
little would be better than nothing. If she didn't tell him where the
blue marble was, he wouldn't let her go. She didn't have to tell him.
She was the only one who knew.

New York again. Trees, then no trees. Streets of buildings. A
slow pace. East Fifty-fifth Street

Con drew up double. "I'll take Griselda up, although we should
be the first here."

He had the keys. She wasn't afraid of the elevator with Con, not of the dark hallway, not of the apartment "I'll be back about six." It was four. "We'll go to dinner. For God's sake, don't let anyone in."

Her eyebrows pointed. "No one? No one?"

"The Montefierrows."

She shivered without knowing it. She chained the doors, leaned out the front window to watch. The mounted patrolman was by the car talking to Tobin. On the desk were a list of calls in Bette's misspells, Ann, Jigg, Gigg, Anna, Artur, Ann.

She luxuriated in bath salts, scrubbed with a sponge of eau de cologne. She groomed herself like a prima ballerina, nails, eyes, hair. It wasn't for Con. He didn't care. He didn't even look at her. It was only to be clean again, clean of the smell of death, of terror. Complete, she didn't dress; zipped herself into coppery lace, copper sandals on her feet.

She called Ann. Ann was so unchanged.

"Where have you been? I've tried and tried to reach you, all day yesterday."

Didn't Ann read the papers? It was black face all over the last night's, this morning's.

Ann went on, "How horrible about Nesta Fahney, wasn't it? And you and Jasper discovering it. But that's where you were, of course. Why did you ever go up there? When are the twins coming back? How awful for them!" She didn't wait for answers. "I want to hear all about it. Can't you come up?"

Griselda breathed, "I'm exhausted. We've just returned. And I'm out to dinner."

"I might come down."

She didn't believe it. Ann never stirred herself.

"I believe I will. Are you busy?"

She sighed. "No. I'm resting. Don't come, Ann. I can't talk about it."

"I'll get a cab and be down right away."

Griselda kicked her heels into the bed. Damn Ann anyway. She'd be there when Con came. She'd spoil everything. Con and Ann filed each other raspingly. She looked over the papers. Pictures of Jasper from the movie files, of Nesta, none of her. The evening papers would have the inquest ones, lights blinding your eyes while you repeated that senseless story.

The doorbell. She opened it on the chain. It was Ann. She closed, reopened, chained it. Ann was unflurried, black with white gloves, white raff on her heavy satin dress.

"Come in the bedroom. I must rest." She lay on the bed.

Ann sat on the edge of it. "Isn't it ghastly? That lovely creature. Tell me."

She repeated again. It began to sound silly, like Peter Rabbit, lippety, lippety. She left out the bad touches. Ann supplied them; she'd read Olga's tabloids.

Griselda told her, "It still makes me rather sick."

"I'm sorry." She asked for a cigarette. "What was Con doing there? Is he back?"

Griselda said yes.

"What are you going to do? Return to the West?"

"I don't know. He may not be staying. He and Tobin drove down with us; they brought me here." Maybe he'd be late and Ann would be gone. She tossed her hair. "I won't move out until he lets me know. I may get some rest yet." She eyed Ann casually. "Anything new on the bank?"

"It's very stupid. Arthur thinks they know but they won't tell anything. Arthur is still working slavishly, checking everything. The police keep asking about a blue marble. What is the blue marble?"

Griselda put her head back on her arms. Heaven knows! But everyone in New York seems hipped on it. I never heard about it on the coast."

The doorbell again. Her watch said six-fifteen. Ann was on her feet "Shall I answer?"

"I'll go." She went quickly, opened the door, forgetting the chain. Those heavy links snapped under a sliver of steel. "Oh!" She put her fist to her mouth, backed away. David and Danny were coming in. David was replacing his stick under his arm. They were as when she first met them, that night. But they weren't smiling now; their eyes were blind. She kept backing and then she caught her breath, said loudly, "Ann's here."

Ann came to the doorway. Griselda didn't dare look away from the twins but her sister's face must have mirrored the pleasure in her voice.

"David! And Danny!"

They smiled then, stopped staring at Griselda.

"Ann, how charming!" They kissed her hands, one on each side. "We didn't expect this surprise!"

Ann's laugh was quicksilver. "Griselda didn't tell me she was dining with you!"

The back of a chair printed Griselda's hand.

Danny laughed. "Are we early, Griselda?"

David took out his cigarette case. "Maybe we could have a drink while Griselda dresses."

She was like a lump of putty.

Ann took David's hand. "I'll help you." She started him to the kitchen.

Then Griselda moved. Her words were shrill. "Yes, do. Fix drinks. I'll dress." She scurried on mice feet, closed the bedroom door behind her, leaned on it. Their voices were light, laughing. She moved, silent as cotton, unleashed the back door, neutralized the bolt, closed it silently behind her. The backstairs weren't frightening now. She fled up to the half floor above, knocked, pounded on the door, her head half-peering below. The door was miraculously opened.

The woman was in black and her mouth had grief blackening it. "What is it? What do you want?"

She didn't let the woman bar her out. She pushed by into that warm, lighted kitchen. She knew that this was Mrs. Grain.

Suspicion poked the words, "Who are you? What do you want?"

Griselda smiled shakily. "May I use your phone?" She couldn't hold the smile. Her voice rattled. "It's terribly important."

Suspicion was there but Mrs. Grain sensed something, something in need. "Well, I guess so. Come along." She led to the ugly living room, stiff with golden oak, garish with framed lithographs and embroidery. "There it is." Decently, she went away.

A telephone. She didn't know whom to call. Where would Con be? She tried headquarters; they gave her Tobin's home number but there was no answer. She tried the broadcasting company, Jasper's rooms, the *Trib*. No one had seen Con; no one had seen Tobin. She couldn't call all the bars in New York.

She put down the phone. Mrs. Grain stood in the door. "Do you want anything else, Miss?"

"No." Hopelessness ravaged her face. "No. That's all. Thank you." She went back through the kitchen, said, "Thank you," again. She was noiseless on the steps. One more chance. She turned to the back apartment, began knocking softly. If only Gig were at home and heard. No answer. She pounded harder and then her fists flattened against that door. She turned trembling.

Danny was there. His lips smiled. He came towards her.

She screamed, pushing against the unyielding door. "Don't touch me!"

He stood a paper breadth away from her. He didn't stop smiling. "Why not?"

Her breath was like wind. "I don't want to die like Nesta Fahney!"

He put his cigarette to his lips, then stepped back. "She was becoming a bore anyway." He beckoned with his head. "Come, get dressed." She followed him like an animal.

2

He shot the bolts, put on the chain, sat down. "Get dressed."

She stood in the middle of the floor. "I won't run again."

The smile had never gone from his lips. "Get dressed."

Red would warm her, hearth-fire red. Clouds of red tulle, red satin for her feet, red roses to circle her hair. Something to warm her, she who would never be warm again. She dressed slowly, preciously, as if for wedding or death. And Danny sat in the chair, smoking, the smile on his mouth, blankness over his eyes. Completion, readjustment of the wreath on her hair, lemon perfume, redder lips. And she heard Con's voice, loud, merry, "Hello, there, having a party!"

So were the condemned reprieved. But she didn't run. She finished her lips, gathered the balloon of black velvet cape over her arm, took velvet gloves and bag. She didn't want to pass Danny's chair. She didn't know what he might do. She forced the red satin slippers to find the connecting door. He stood, followed her.

"Con." Her throat was steady.

He didn't like Danny coming out of her room. A flash in his eyes. She ignored it.

"You're late, darling." She was trivial, touched his arm. To the others, "You'll excuse us rushing you off. We've a dinner engagement."

Ann was puzzled. The twins were civilized. Ann began, "I thought…"

David put his smile on. "Thanks for the drinks, Griselda." Their hats tilted, white scarfs knotted. "Coming with us, Ann?"

She looked at Con, at Griselda. "Yes. I hadn't realized how late it is."

Tricklings but they were gone at last and Griselda stood, her fingers pressing her cheeks, as if to force away memory.

Con looked her over. "What the hell?"

She began picking up glasses, emptying ash trays.

He repeated the question.

"You are taking me to dinner, aren't you? You said you were." Her voice shook.

He eyed her with curiosity. "Sure I am. But why the get-up? You know how I love a stiff collar."

She fingered the tulle. "You don't even have to shave, or change your shirt." And then she began to cry without sound or meaning.

He was sharp "Cut it, babe. What's up?"

She couldn't say anything. He didn't touch her. "I'll shave." He went into the bedroom. She tagged after, sat quietly in the chair where Danny had been. She was afraid to be alone.

He pulled out his dinner clothes.

She cried out, "You needn't!"

"I'm not a heel. Think I take a pretty girl out looking like one?" He whistled while he dressed. "Besides I'm not so bad looking my-self when I get dolled up." He was whistling an old song; they'd sung it five years ago. "'Every star above…' Maybe not as fancy as your twinnies but not bad." He transferred keys, books, pencils, polished his shoes with a towel, hung his hat on his head. "Come on, hon." He billowed the cape around her. "Thought I told you to look out for Montefierrows."

They were at the door. She touched the broken chain. "They

came in." She remembered their eyes, their advance. She began to tremble again, forced rigidity. Her laugh wasn't real. "Lucky Ann was here."

There was a small restaurant down below on Fifty-sixth. It smelled of the sea and French sauces. They sat in the corner on padded leather, their backs to the wall.

He passed cigarettes, asked, "You haven't smoked any of the twins' brand?"

"No. They've never offered them."

"Don't. Tobin had stubs tested. There are two varieties, one to stimulate the nerves, one to still the nerves."

She'd been suspicious.

He asked the inevitable question. "Where is the blue marble?"

She was silent. He repeated.

She said, "I won't tell you that."

He shoved the salt shaker away. "Why not? Suppose something happens to you. Does anyone know?"

She said that no one did.

"Well then?"

"If anything happens to me, you'll get it."

"Why not tell me now?"

She raised her eyes to him. "It's better you don't know."

"Mm?"

"You're safer not knowing."

He put his head back, chuckled, "You're protecting me?"

She nodded, solemn eyes on him.

He cocked his head suddenly. "I do believe you've still got a heart for me."

She looked away, "What if I have?"

"No." He tossed it away. "No. You divorced me. You knew how worthless I was. You told me so. For once you were right. And I haven't improved during the years."

M'sieur's waiters began loading the table with fish. Food ended conversation. When dinner had quieted her, she asked, "Are you going back to the border?"

He made a negative noise, swallowed Bourbon. "Not till this is washed up."

She wanted to know. She didn't know how to ask.

He thought of it too. "You needn't get out, if you don't mind me bunking with you." He was the extreme of casualness.

"I don't mind. I wouldn't stay there alone now." She kept her voice steady. Then she did look at him. "What about Gig? The one I call Gig."

He looked at her too. The moment was gone. "I don't know. I'll keep out of sight until you let him know I'm back. We'll see what he does."

She was irrelevant. "He's nice." She didn't want him hurt. He'd been on her side.

"Mm." His mouth was full.

They were dawdling. The dishes had vanished.

"Want to go to a show?"

"No, thank you."

He yawned. "Better go home then. Toby wants to see you tomorrow."

"Again?" She was tired of all this.

"Yeah." He beckoned a cab. He didn't believe in walking a block. "There's some things you know that you ought to tell."

"Maybe."

They were at home. It was safe not to be going in alone, opening that elevator alone, riding with terror.

"You're still going to hold out on the marble?"

She nodded.

He swung the useless chain. "Better get a new one tomorrow."

"What good will it do?"

He scratched his head. "That's right." He moved an end table against the door, set a lamp on the ragged edge of it, put a glass of water on top of the lamp. He chortled, "At least we'll be warned."

Her lips curved. She went to the bedroom, began undressing. He passed through, began washing his teeth. It was like being married again only he was polite now, not in love with her. She got into bed with the evening papers. She couldn't read much with her glasses somewhere in Mexico. The inquest photos were absurd. Jasper looked like an old man. She looked like a scared pullet.

Con came in rubbing his jaws. She asked him without looking up from the newsprint, "When do I get my glasses? I shouldn't read without them."

He was examining his nails. "I forgot. I'll talk to the fellows tomorrow. They ought to be down by then. When's the funeral?"

"Private services here Saturday. The big stuff in Hollywood."

He got in bed, took half the papers. They read in silence. She put out her lamp. He went on reading. She closed her eyes.

He asked, "You don't mind my staying here?"

She didn't open them "Not at all."

It was like marriage, only different.

3

He was snoring when she woke. The phone shrilled, the door banged. She shook him, "Answer the door, Con." It was nine-thirty. She took the phone.

Ann said, "I want to talk to you, Griselda. Will you lunch with me?" She sounded troubled.

She was a little suspicious. "You'll be alone?"

"Yes. Of course." She hung up, went to the doorway. Con was

clattering in the kitchen. He said, "It was the cleaner." She returned to the bedroom, dressed with elegance for courage. A pencil of black crepe with shaggy hyacinth flowers under the chin. Her hat was a flung sail. At the living room door again she asked, "Isn't Bette here yet?"

Con was humped on the couch, drinking something amber. He yawned, "That's funny, she isn't."

"You shouldn't drink so early, Con."

"All right, babe." He finished the glass.

She told him, "I'll be at Ann's for lunch."

"Think it's safe?"

"She said alone." Her eyebrows narrowed. "I can't understand Bette not being here. She must be sick."

Con said, "Call me later."

4

Ann herself opened the door. "I'm glad you could come. I needed you today."

They went through the French doors to the dining room. There were jonquils bright in a round silver vase. Olga served shrimp, chilled sliced tomatoes.

Griselda was surprised to be ravenous. "What did you do last night?"

Ann's eyes brightened. "We went to an amazing little French place for dinner, way downtown. I have a problem, Griselda." She flickered at the closed door of the serving pantry, lowered her voice. "David wants me to drive up to the country with him this week end. Do you suppose Arthur would mind?"

Griselda's throat was tight. "Don't go!"

Ann showed her surprise.

She made it matter-of-fact "Of course Arthur would mind."

"But there's no reason for him to know." She was a child pleading the cause of green apples. "He has to go to Washington tomorrow on bank business. He won't be back until Sunday night."

She pleaded now, "Don't go, Ann. Arthur wouldn't like it. Those things are always found out. You know that."

Ann wasn't quite truthful and she knew it. She was almost pious, Ann in her violet velvet hostess gown, her fingers tipped with mauve red. "But, Griselda, you surely don't think I mean anything wrong! There's nothing like that. It isn't going away with a man for the week end." She perished the thought! "I'd merely be their guest, nothing uncivilized."

Griselda shook her head. "It isn't that." How to tell Ann and not tell her, how to frighten what lived under the precious lacquer mask. "Listen to me, Ann. You remember that night at the Persian room."

"Which night?"

"When the twins were with us."

Ann did remember. It came a shadow into the pupils of her eyes, was pushed back into the beyond of things not to be remembered, not ever to think upon. "What are you talking about, Griselda? You always did have the queerest ideas."

Griselda sighed. You couldn't put things across to Ann obliquely. She understood but would continue to refuse. That was the why of Ann; she was as she was, nurtured, masked, because she would see and understand only that which she wished.

They moved into the living room. Griselda flopped into the yellow quilted chair. You couldn't tell Ann in indirect motion, why did she try? Because she didn't want Ann hurt, although it would serve her right to be hurt, badly, in the face of such stubbornness. But Ann was her sister, beautiful if empty, too normal to be put to death, or worse, to be put to use as was Missy. She struggled again. "You don't want to be murdered in your bed, Ann."

Ann didn't stir from her pose on the laureled couch. But the fingers on her velvet skirt rose and slowly fell. "No, I don't, Griselda." She raised her eyelids. "I don't fear that. I trust David."

Griselda spoke slowly. "Of them all I too trust David. I don't believe he kills." If only she could put this much across to Ann. "But there is such a thing as arousing the Furies."

Now Ann did stir. She was not comfortable. And the mask went away from her face. She leaned towards Griselda, whispered it. "Who killed Nesta Fahney?"

Griselda saw that room again, saw it so horribly that Ann's couch became an old white-iron bedstead; the green laurel, dried blood. She put her fingers to her eyes.

Fright shrilled the whisper now. "Who killed Nesta Fahney?"

Griselda stared at her sister with empty eyes. Beneath the lipstick Ann's mouth had the color of quince. Griselda continued to stare with a child's curiosity at the elder; she had never before seen Ann without blood and bones, nothing but a flabby shape. This was fear, stark horrible fear. She wondered if this was as she herself had been that day in the farmhouse room, that night in the bank, that other when Mr. Grain spilled blood on Con's carpet, and that first night when the twins spoke to her on the corner of Fifty-fifth and Fifth. She shivered. This had been going on for many years; it would go on forever, as long as the twins…

"Who killed Nesta Fahney?"

She answered without meaning, "I don't know."

Whispering again. "Did Missy kill her?" There was nothing of Ann but eyes, not eyes, round black pupils. The rest of her was gone.

Griselda repeated, "I don't know."

Those black circles were furied from fear, that sightless panic of fear. "You do know. You were there. You saw her. Did Missy kill her?"

She repeated, "I don't know." And then she broke out again with, "Don't go up there with David, Ann. Don't do it. It isn't for you." But her pleading only made Ann come to life again, the Cheshire eyes filling out with cheekbone, head, shoulders, thighs, green velvet sandals.

The lovely masked Ann was there again, putting her ivory cigarette holder to her lips, saying, "I don't know as yet what I will do, Griselda. I may go. It might be amusing. And then again..." The fear went down into dark again, but there was left a shadow of it, something that wouldn't go away so soon.

Under her breath Griselda kept repeating, urging, "Don't go. Don't go. Don't go." But not aloud. Too much dissent and Ann would go.

Arthur was interruption. He came in on his key, looking important, broad. He kissed Ann's dark hair, not as Con would kiss. Arthur's lips made habit, not emotion. She half-spoke, "You're early. Are you still going to Washington?"

"Yes, in the morning."

Griselda mentioned, "Ann said bank business. Anything more on it?"

He was so important. "Well, yes and no. At any rate Tobin thought it would be wise if we'd talk to Barjon Garth."

He pretended to be everyday but he wasn't. It was something to be going to Washington to see the famous X head.

Her pretense was better. She took a brown wafer from Ann's always-filled china box, nibbled it. "Just what's it about? Or is it secret?"

"Well, we don't care to have it in the press, naturally. There'd be a hullabaloo. But Tobin thinks if we went through the deposit boxes, there might be some clue. He wants Garth's advice."

She could hide her fear, sucking at the chocolate. Only one box Tobin wanted to touch.

"Temporarily we've placed a guard at the vault. Nothing is to be removed from it without a record."

"Won't that cause trouble?"

"No, indeed," he said. "Everyone has been most co-operative."

And naturally. Anyone with legitimate business would be co-operative. If it weren't legitimate—no one would go to the vault now. She couldn't go. But Con must not see that letter. She flushed. It had been foolish to tell in it how she felt about him. Not that that really mattered now; humiliation was as nothing. But if Con took the marble, the twins would move against him.

She finished the chocolate, wiped her fingers on her tongue. "I'd better run. I must see Gig. He must have wondered about me."

"I like him," Arthur decided. "Something solid about him."

Always, either of them, undermining Con, but they couldn't. Con was Con, beloved, even if he scorned social graces, social lines.

She looked straight at Ann. "Call me." It was a command. Her sister understood.

"Yes, I promise I'll call you."

Arthur saw her to the door. She went down, out into the cold sunshine. She walked the block over to Fifth, skirted down towards the shining towers. Buses elephanted down the street but she didn't hail them. Walking was better. It made her head clear; it let air into her lungs. She hadn't breathed for so many days. Tomorrow the twins would go upstate again. Or was it to be only Ann and David? What did David want with Ann? Merely diversion? But he was not Danny; women were nothing to him. Did he want Ann for another reason, to take Missy's place? Griselda was colder than the breath frosting from her mouth. Had Missy bungled things slaughtering Nesta? Had she outworn her use? And Ann, cool, casual Ann, without emotion, would she fit better into their mold—with the help of those drugged cigarettes?

"She shivered in the sunlight. They couldn't do it to Ann. No, they actually couldn't. She walked briskly again. They didn't know. Ann's civilization would defeat them. She would do nothing that kept her from being invited to the Potters and the Van Rensaellers and the Kingdoms. They couldn't offer anything good enough to take the place of the right invitations. The very qualities that would make Ann valuable to them were those which would keep her out of their madness. But what did David want with Ann? Surely not for Ann to die. That didn't make reason. And they couldn't think that Ann was in any way tied up with the blue marble. That was impossible.

She couldn't figure it. There was something more important to her. Con must not read the letter, know where to find the marble. She would give it up first. She didn't know what to do. She only knew she must keep free until Arthur brought Garth's decision. Only if she were free to get that letter first would Con stay safe. She crossed the width of Fifty-seventh, two blocks to Fifty-fifth, turned, but she turned back again to Fifth, rounding the corner with even, unhurried steps. Was that Tobin down the block, down by No. 21, idling before the window where there was an old Chinese vase and two tapestries? There was no other hat like to that. Tobin, looking towards Madison. Usually Griselda came from Ann's on the Mad. bus. Tobin, waiting to spy her, to pretend casual meeting? But nothing was casual now. Suppose he had come to arrest her! Panic seized her. She couldn't go home. She could go to Gig.

XIII

SHE HAILED a cab. "Columbia." She held tight to the edge of the seat as they bounced up Broadway to One Hundred Sixteenth Street. The driver let her off at the corner and she pushed a bill into his hand, not waiting change. She didn't know which of these buildings but there was a boy smoking on the steps. He directed her.

She asked at the registrar's window. "J. Antwerp Gigland."

The girl stared at her strangely. "He isn't here."

"Not here?"

"No." That strange look again, then the girl said anxiously, "Wouldn't you like to sit down? You look ill."

Griselda tried to smile. "I'm all right. Only I was surprised. When did he leave?"

"He's been away about a month. Dr. Wilkes Gigland is taking his classes. Would he—could he help you?"

She said, "I'll see him." She followed directions, to that first red brick building, up in the creeping elevator. The certain office; inside was Gig.

He too looked at her so strangely, pulling forward a chair. "Griselda, sit here. What's happened? I've been trying to reach you. Your sister said you hadn't been in."

"Ann said that?" Was all the world crazy?

"Not Ann. The other one. At Con's."

"Oh." She touched her throat. Missy had been there, was there. Why?

He was calm. "What has happened, Griselda?"

She held his hands, tightly. "I don't know. I'm in a funk, Gig. I want to run away, and I can't now. I'm in it too deeply."

"Let's get out of here," he said. "Go where we can talk. To my apartment."

She shook her head. "I don't dare. Tobin's outside. And Missy's already there." Everything closing in. She couldn't breathe.

He put on his hat, coat. He was gentle. He rested you. Even if he weren't Gig. She asked, "Are you Gig's brother—J. Antwerp Gigland?"

He flushed. "I'm his cousin. I should have told you." He was so embarrassed. "But I didn't think you'd be interested. You had your own troubles."

"Where's Gig? Con's Gig I mean."

He said, "He had a chance to go to Persia on a survey. He asked me to take his place. It was arranged at the University. I'd been teaching in Germany, before things changed there…"

It didn't matter.

He opened the door. "I suppose they told you at the office when you asked for him."

She said, "Yes—I…" She, mustn't say she knew it before, that would give Con away. "I asked by the full name." She even laughed. "I don't know why."

They went down in the elevator. He asked, "If you don't go home, where will you stay?"

"I don't know." No place was safe.

"Why can't we smuggle you into my place? We could do it. No one need know. You'd be near home to get clothes and things." He thought of a way. "The fire escape. The back apartments have them. I'll go up in the elevator and open the window."

They did it. She standing below in the dirty, dank courtyard, her heart in her mouth, until his head stuck out four stories above. She climbed the damp treachery of the old iron ladder. No one saw. And she was inside, rubbing her hands together for warmth.

"You're safe here. Why don't you take a hot bath? That would relax you, maybe sleep. I've papers to correct. I won't leave until you're awake. You'll be safe with me here."

"Yes." There was much he hadn't explained but maybe it was true. Whether he was safe or not, she felt comfortable with him. She went into the bedroom, closed the door.

When she woke it was dark. But light shone under the door from the living room where Gig was working. Or was he gone? She put on the lamp, opened the door a crack. He was there and alone, but the gate-leg table was loaded with food.

He saw her. "I called L'Apértif and asked for service for two." He blushed. "I believe the waiter thought I was having a rendezvous."

She patted his shoulder. "You're an angel. And I do feel better." She was rested, ravenous, almost gay. She ate hungrily. "I don't believe I've really tasted food in a week. I'm not scared now. How long do you think I'll be safe here?"

"Until someone finds out. And why should anyone find out? I can bring in food, do your telephoning. You stay away from doors, windows and phones; you should be safe enough."

"Bette?"

He was surprised she didn't know. "She won't be coming. She was shot."

"Not…" She couldn't speak it.

He shook his head. "Her arm, I believe. I found her. In your apartment. She's all right. Griselda, don't look so distressed. But she won't be here for some days."

"I could do her cleaning for exercise."

They laughed a little then finished dinner almost in silence.

Over cigarettes her eyebrows folded together. "It is important that I reach Con. He must know where I am. You don't know him, do you?"

He was embarrassed again. "I've met him with my cousin. I doubt if he'd remember."

"If you saw him?"

"I'd know him, yes."

She said, "You write a note, leave it in his box. Say: 'Con, get in touch with Gig immediately. Important.'"

He wrote. "Shall I take it down now?"

"Yes. Here…" She handed him the key to the box. "Take your door key with you too and let yourself in. I won't open the door. If there's mail for me, will you bring it?"

He nodded.

She wasn't ill at ease with him away. She smoked quietly until he returned. He brought a note in Con's writing. It had been dropped in the box, not mailed. "Be good a day or so. Watch your step." The heart went out of her again. She flung it towards Gig, sat down. She laughed, uncertain. "He may be in Chapala by now. With Con you never know."

He read it, looked at her, touched it "Anything I can do, Griselda? You know I'd do anything for you."

She was silent, wondering. "Dear Gig." But she couldn't ask him to break into a bank vault for her. And suppose it were not true, his simple explanation of two Gigs. Suppose the other Gig, the real one, were somewhere face down in a pool of blood. She shuddered. "No. No, Gig."

He spoke softly. "You needn't be afraid—for me."

She touched his hand. "I know. But you've involved yourself enough as it is, Gig. Too much. There's nothing more you can do. Give me something hard to read while you're at your night class. Maybe that will put me to sleep again."

He handed her "The Art of Weaving in Medieval Persia," presenting it with a sweeping bow.

2

Gig was, of course, gone in the morning. He'd left the papers, food in the icebox, the percolator ready to be plugged. It would be a peaceful day, not to be fleeing from one place to another. It was ten o'clock before she got up, rolled her pajama sleeves, took broom and mop, and emulated the good Bette. She would have liked to sing but that might be heard; further, despite her carefree spirit, something was listening for the whine of the elevator.

She washed the breakfast things. Everything spandy. Then she dressed lazily; it was nearing noon. And then she remembered— Ann! She took up the phone. She couldn't reach the operator; the line was dead. It would happen now. She'd have to risk going out. She put on coat and hat, took her bag, gloves.

She couldn't open the front door. She wrestled it; it wouldn't open. She stood soundless, then tried again, in panic now, but it was fast. It took all her courage to attempt the back way. That door also would not budge. She was locked in.

Had Gig done this? Was it so she could not get away; was the telephone no accident but that she could not communicate? She couldn't believe that; she wouldn't. The phone an accident; the doors for her own safety.

There was a way out, the fire escape, or was that barred too? No way to shut off that escape. Had he thought she wouldn't dare go that way? The danger of being seen—but she had to risk it. She opened the window, peered below. There was no one in sight. She stepped out, pulled the window after her, hearing as she did the whine of the ascending elevator. You couldn't hurry on those precarious iron rods. It took hours to climb down, expecting every moment sound from above, a window opened, to be caught.

She took the leap to the ground. She didn't dare emerge the front way. She crossed through another court, through dirty passageways, out on Fifty-sixth Street Whether to go towards Fifth or Madison, she didn't know. The Mad. buses were faster but Tobin had been watching Madison yesterday. She was afraid of cabs. She half-ran to Fifth, caught a bus, chafed at traffic delays. At Seventy-eighth she got off, walked up the block and looked carefully down Seventy-ninth before almost fleeing towards the apartment house. It was surprising that the doorman should be the same one; she'd never really noticed his face before; it was round and ruddy, kind. And the elevator man, dark and square, looked as if he had a wife and children. Olga seemed surprised to see her.

"Mrs. Stepney?"

Olga didn't close the door quickly enough. You were safe only with doors closed and bolted. Griselda took the knob from the maid's hand, put her back against its shutness.

"Mrs. Stepney?"

By the girl's eyes, she knew the answer.

"But she left early, Miss Satterlee."

Griselda's fingers were clenched. "Did she say…"

"To the country with friends."

"Did she say when she would return?"

"Sometime tomorrow, she thinks. Or Monday morning."

This was Saturday. She remembered then something else. Services for Nesta. Private, but that only meant greater hordes of fans. She wouldn't be missed by the fans but Oppy and Jasper would know. The press would know. The police would wonder? Surely it would be safe to pay last tribute. The Montefierrows wouldn't be there. Not if Ann had gone away with them. If she went with Oppy and Jasper she'd be safe.

She called the Waldorf. The clerk said Mr. Coldwater would speak with no one, doctor's orders. She told him with cold fury, "This is Griselda Satterlee. Get me through to Mr. Coldwater or Mr. Oppensterner or you'll never have another celebrity at your hotel!" She hadn't the nerves for tact now.

Jasper was speaking. "What is it, Griselda? You've no idea what I've been through. It's positively revolting. I am exhausted. Where are you? Oppy's been trying to reach you. The services are at three."

She told him, "I'm at my sister's, Ann's. Can you come for me?"

"Griselda!" He shrieked it. "If you knew! I can't even put my head out of the door. We have guards. The fans!"

She said, "I can't help that, Jasper. I suppose I have to be there today. And I can't go alone."

He spoke aside for the moment, then said, "We'll send for you."

She told him flatly, "I don't trust anyone I don't know. Whom can you send?"

He mentioned Jack Churchill, one of Oppy's publicists. That was satisfactory.

She warned him, "Don't tell anyone else where I am."

He was weary. "I wouldn't dream of it, Griselda. They've been hounding you, too. I know how it is."

He didn't know. He wasn't in danger. But she could trust Jack. She added, "Tell him to come up for me."

He said yes. "Wear a heavy veil. Women are fortunate. They can wear veils."

She had lunch on a tray, then finger-tapped until Olga announced him. It couldn't have been long, long as it seemed; they were before time for the services. The walks in front of the fashionable church were packed, police lines holding the gogglers back.

Jasper said: Wear a veil, as if Ann's wardrobe held mourning veils. But no one would know her face. She wasn't of this; she was an innocent bystander. Churchill took her arm through the guard lines, down the church aisle. She was to sit with Jappy and Oppy. They rose to let her enter the pew.

Jasper whispered, "I'm exhausted. What I've been through! You've no idea!" but he kept his face looking doleful.

The organ was sad, and the preacher's poignant words in a more poignant voice. Gardenias, Nesta's flower, were blooming everywhere; the scent was overpowering, nauseous. Everyone was sniffling and fat tears rolled down Oppy's cheeks, plopping on his derby. But it wasn't sad about Nesta. There was nothing for which she should continue existence except more money and more clothes and more men. It was sad about Mr. Grain, and his wife so lone; about the bank guard with never a chance. Nesta had walked into her own web. But everyone wept as if something beautiful and lovely had been halted.

Not everyone. Not Jasper, strong and silent, beating back tears. Not Tobin two pews ahead and across, but the back of his head looked at her. Not Moore, two pews back; you could see him when you looked towards Oppy. Nor Griselda, wondering why they were here, frightened of them now because they could balk her freedom.

The organ played recessional and everyone stood up. Jasper whispered, still lugubrious, "We're flying back this afternoon. You'd better come too."

Escape. If she could. But she couldn't. She said, "I can't, Jasper. I wish I might." The passion of regret took away his feigned sorrow for the moment and he peered curiously at her.

"You'd better come, Griselda. I'd be afraid to stay around here any longer. Too many queer things happening." He half-shivered.

They were in the aisle, Oppy first, Jasper and she, in single file moving slowly to the door. Fresh air, out of the stifle of gardenia scent.

She spoke a word to Oppy, poor little red-nosed Oppy, and Jasper playing to the now-sobbing sidewalk starers.

Oppy wept, "You won't go with us to the airport? There will be photographers there, and we will scatter Cape jasmines." He said it jas-o-mines. "All the way to California! That's better than gardenias, everybody has gardenias." He blew his nose.

She said, "It will be wonderful, Oppy. You do things right. But I can't go." She watched them leave, Tobin and Moore leading in an official car. She was left alone in the hordes of strangers, feeling a forlorn and frightened waif.

There was no place for her to go, no place to lay her head. Suppose Tobin had taken her away in that car. Suppose the twins should close in on her now, or Missy, with a hatchet in her hand. Gig might take her, lock her in again. The panic that had been hers all day surged now unbearably. She'd have to hide away to stay safe for Con. Other people hid in New York. She would go to a hotel. But she wanted her own things, a change of clothes. It was reckless but it should be perfectly safe now, the police at the airport, Gig at the University, the twins in the country. She would hasten.

There was no one in sight when she slipped in. She opened the apartment door, closed it noiselessly, and started to the coat closet for her grip. She stopped short. The door to it was ajar, someone lying in the shadows there as if he'd fallen face down out of the darkness. It wasn't Con; she could see that. Somehow this didn't shock her, perhaps she was beyond that now; nor, strangely enough, was she frightened. She bent over, and then she saw placed near the hand, as if he were reaching for them, her glasses. She knew who it was. Without thought she retrieved her glasses, put them on. She knew she must get away, get away fast now.

She went into the bedroom. The bag of Con's in the closet was too big but no way to get her own. She packed more than she needed, another dress, another; change of shoes, hats with tissue paper crumpled in their hollows. But she couldn't delay too long. She must go away; she must go fast. It was as if childhood was returned; you could put off taking the medicine but not forever.

She wasn't afraid to go through the living room but she didn't. She went the back way, once terror to her, through the areaway to the front curb. The heavy bag bumped her knees. She must await a cab. And then behind her she heard the voice.

"I thought you'd forgotten me."

The dark laughing face with the black eyes, the stick pointed. He'd come from within the apartment foyer. She might have known it was impossible. She couldn't hope to get away.

A town car, black, unobtrusively elegant, was drawn up at the curb. There was nothing to do but precede him.

She asked, "Why are you taking me to Queechy?"

"Any number of reasons." He was lighting one of his cigarettes. She wondered, was it depressive or exciting? "This is end of the story. We will have the marble and leave."

She parroted, "I don't have the blue marble."

He sucked smoke. "We have about come to that conclusion, Griselda. But we will know soon." There was nothing of menace in the way he spoke but something twitched, warned her.

"You will know. How will you know?" The dark buildings rushed by, trees were beginning to grow on the roadways.

He said, "We'll know from Con."

She was frightened. "Con has nothing to do with it."

"Don't be absurd. We know Con had the marble. You say you don't have it. It follows, he has it."

She wanted time to think. "Why take me to the country then?"

"He will follow you."

She could laugh. "What makes you think so?"

"Dear stupid child." He laughed. "If you have the marble he will come in order that you do not give it away." He shrugged. "If you haven't it, he will come anyway for you."

"You're the stupid one, David. Con doesn't care what happens to me."

"No? You don't love each other?"

"No, we don't." Her eyes were wide. "We're divorced."

"What do words matter? He'll come for you. He's in love with you. I know these things. I see them. He won't let you rot with us. And if you were to be in danger, he would come quickly. When he comes we will see about the marble."

He was wrong, but not wrong that Con would come, stick his head into it because of the damned marble. Danger. He had said that before when she was thinking of Con. Danger. The word didn't have the bright sound that poets gave to it. It was something dark and furry, nauseous.

David said, "Rest if you can. It's quite a way, you know. We won't hurry. We'll stop for dinner." It was growing dark.

She couldn't sleep, not with him there. She questioned suddenly, frightened again, "Ann?"

"She's quite all right. Even enjoying her stay."

"Why did you want Ann?" She demanded it.

"Perhaps I couldn't get out of inviting her." He laughed.

She didn't believe him.

She did drowse a little, not into the deep mesh of sleep, but on the surface hammock. She opened her eyes to a lane of intertwining trees, then a glimmer of water. It was dark now.

He said, "We are there."

The car stopped. He opened the door, stepped out, his stick pointing towards her. "This way, Griselda."

She felt her way under the lacings of trees, down a stony path, touching his shoulders for guidance. He walked as a night thing, even as she had noticed before.

The cottage to which he led was two-storied, with a screened porch below and above. It stood on a hilly place, the lake gray, soft-spoken, at its feet. There was a yellow spill of light from the windows. The other cottages at angles right and left and beyond were dark as they were silent.

He spoke briefly as they went up the wooden steps to the porch. "Do not frighten Ann."

She whispered, "No. We must not frighten Ann."

He opened the door into the glow of the living room. Missy was curled on the flowered couch. Danny had a drink before the burning fireplace. Both looked at her.

Danny said sourly, "You were long enough."

David nodded. "Yes. I was. Get us a drink, Missy."

She uncurled. She seemed tiny, somehow pathetic, like a child in her pink coat and silk pajama legs. Her eyes weren't pathetic. They were hot, as sun on a mirror. "Did she bring it?" Her words, were greedy.

Danny said, "Missy, darling, our guest desires a drink," and David helped Griselda with her coat. She sat in the chair opposite Danny by the fireplace, surprised at her chill, her tiredness. She took the glass from Missy's hand, looked curiously into it, then at her sister.

Missy was cross-legged at Danny's feet. "It won't hurt you. There's no poison in it."

Griselda looked at her evenly. "No, that isn't your weapon."

Something licked in Missy's eyes. She leaned her shoulders against Danny's shins. He put his hand on her lemon hair.

David drew up another chair. "Don't bother Griselda now. She's had a long trip. She needs sleep before we discuss matters."

She thanked him ironically, sipped her drink. Then she asked,

"I suppose it's no news to you that Irish Galvatti has been murdered?"

The twins opened their blank eyes wide and Missy spat an unprintable word.

Danny bristled laughter. "Missy is such a jealous child."

Griselda was too tired to feel. She set down the drink. David said, "I'll take you upstairs. You share with Ann. We're rather crowded here."

Missy yawned. "Beastly place."

She said, "Goodnight," and pointedly, "I hope this will be a quiet night."

David assured her courteously, "Nothing will disturb your slumbers, Griselda." She followed him up the staircase. He tapped at the right hand door. Ann's voice sounded, nervous, "Who...?"

He nodded to Griselda.

She answered, "It's I, Ann. Griselda."

David went downstairs before the key turned in the lock.

3

It was a large double bed. The door was re-locked, a chair placed under the knob.

Ann whispered, "I'm so glad you've come, Griselda. They said you were coming but I didn't believe."

"They said that?"

"Yes, but you didn't." Ann sighed under the sheet. "And now you are here. I don't even mind sharing the bed, and I much prefer sleeping alone." Her voice was softer than a whisper. "I'm sorry you came but I'm glad. You understand? I've been—so—so disturbed."

Griselda held her breath. "What's happened?"

"Nothing." It was hard for Ann to speak. She wasn't accustomed to being out of her gilded theater. "Nothing you can say, Griselda. I don't know." Then tensely, "Have you ever seen their eyes, Griselda?"

"Whose eyes?" But she knew.

"The twins. Have you ever noticed? You can't see into them."

"Yes. I've noticed that." She tried to make it usual, natural. "Is that what's frightened you?"

"No. I tell you it's nothing. And then, Missy and Danny—they've been quarreling horribly, Griselda, horribly…"

"They aren't pleasant." She wanted to quiet Ann, to keep Ann out of this.

"Why did you come here?"

"I don't know. Really I don't, Griselda. David kept urging, and I was bored. He is—was—attractive."

"Why did they want you here?"

Ann stirred the bed shaking her head. "I don't know. I really don't know. But they took the key to my apartment. I know one of them did. It was in my purse when I came and it isn't there now. And they've asked and asked questions about you."

She broke in, "What questions?"

"If you stayed at my apartment at all, if you left anything there. Do you know what I think? I think they're still looking for that blue marble."

"I think you're right," Griselda told her softly. Key or no key, she wasn't afraid they'd found it.

"I wanted to get word to you not to come, or to bring Arthur when you did. But I couldn't. There's no phone, and I couldn't get away."

"Couldn't?" The echo was cautious.

Ann's voice shook a little. "They watch all the time. They pretend they don't but they know every moment where you are, what you are doing. I tried to get away this afternoon when I was frightened after David left. I don't suppose I would have gone really. But I thought if I reached a main road I might stop a car. I started out to the road, the one that comes in here, and Danny was there. He asked where I was going."

"What did you tell him?"

"That I was taking a little stroll. And he said, 'Let's stroll this way.' He took my arm and—I went with him. I was afraid not to, Griselda."

They heard footfalls climbing the stairs, more than, one; past the door, down the corridor. Ann was stretched like a wire in the bed. They heard a door close.

Ann whispered, her whisper almost too soft to be audible. "And Missy. I'm even afraid of Missy, Griselda. Isn't that absurd? Our own sister and the baby, too. But she came on the porch this evening. Danny and I were sitting there, and she looked—I can't tell you."

Griselda spoke with urgency. "Don't be alone with Danny, Ann."

"I don't want to be alone with any of them. I want to go back home. Why do you suppose they're keeping us here?"

She wanted to be helpful. "They'll tire of this place soon. I think they are waiting for Con now. It's getting' late. I must sleep."

Ann said, lonely, "I wish I could sleep."

4

Through all of life, she would never forget this. The three lithe bodies stretching upwards on the raft against the sun, leaping together into the golden-drenched waters. Even although she knew they were only waiting to kill her too, they were beautiful, so beautiful they hurt. She dived from the shore dock, stung with the shock of cold, came up gasping and ran, robed in red wool, back to Ann by the fire.

She said, "I think they're coming in now."

Ann didn't look up to speak. "There isn't a scrap of paper, no letters, notes, nothing, in any of their belongings. There isn't anything personal. It's as if all three of them were just delivered outright from some shop."

Griselda said on the stairs, "Thanks for looking. I know you hated it."

"I didn't mind." She followed Griselda. "It's better than just sitting here shivering."

They heard the others come in while Griselda pulled on her cream sweater, zipped the scarlet, black and white skirt. They returned to the living room below.

Griselda asked, "What do we do about food?"

Ann returned to pretense of the magazine. "There's some deaf old woman comes in to cook and a little dusting. She never says a word."

Danny and Missy came tumbling down the steps. David was behind them. They were like an interlude in a musical piece, all in slacks, moccasins, blue-white sweat shirts. Missy was singing, some little French taunt. It was all high-spirited, as if this were in reality but a pleasure trip. Missy sat in the exact center of the rug and lit one of her tiny cigarettes. She shook the daisy petals of her bright head. "Next week we will be sailing on the ocean again. Won't it be so lovely, Danny? Water under our heels."

David said, "I wouldn't smoke too much, Missy."

Her purple eyes were wide, childlike. "I've not smoked since breakfast."

"You promised," he reminded her quietly.

"I'll be good, very good. Just this one?"

Ann put down the magazine. "When do you plan to start back to the city, David?" She was casual, so casual. "Arthur will be back tonight, or certainly tomorrow morning."

"He'll be delayed."

The magazine slid to the floor, each page's rustle louder than if a tray of dishes had crashed. "Delayed?" Ann's question was terrored, so soft, softer than a pillow.

Missy looked straight at her, then deliberately giggled, and Ann's terror was as lightning over her face. Griselda crossed to her, pretending to go nearer the fire, pumping the spirit of her strength into the older sister.

"The business took longer?"

David stilled the fear that was whispering. "Unfortunately yes."

Ann didn't say anything.

Griselda went from her again, to the windows where you might see the quiet of the lake. The twins didn't want delay now. Did they know the X division was on their heels? Had they made a mistake? But not even the X could stop the twins. If Con came she'd make him see the foolishness of keeping up this game, make him give up the marble. It wasn't right to keep it until everyone died. Not even to trap the twins.

She laughed, seeing the world ending, bit by bit, while the twins searched on and on for the very blue marble. She felt Danny's head turn at the laugh and she was rigid again. She'd make Con see it; she'd make him, knowing how impossible it was to make Con do anything he didn't believe. But if he didn't see it, she'd give them the blue marble anyway, fling it in their faces, get rid of them, anything to make them go away. Until they were gone there could be no peace again, nothing usual.

Ann was foolish. She had to shatter the quiet which David had so kindly given. "When will we go back to the city?"

Danny yawned. "Aren't you enjoying your visit?"

Griselda turned sharply. Ann's back was harsh against their chair.

David said, "Don't be disturbing, Ann. We can't go yet. We've other guests coming, you know."

"Others?" She shouldn't have such pitying fear in each word, each look. Griselda walked to the fire against the chair.

"Yes. Con's coming. Or so the twins say."

"We hope so," David admitted. "We might have food. Missy, ask that creature why it isn't ready."

Missy lay flat on the rug, her knees in the air. "Why don't you?"

He told her, "I can't bear to look at her ugly face."

Missy said, "I always get the hard work." She rolled over on her stomach, then jumped up.

Danny must have done it deliberately. He could have waited until she was in the kitchen. He knew she hadn't even opened the door. He yawned and stretched again, stood and crossed to Ann. "You're bored. So am I. We'll take a walk this afternoon, shall we?"

Ann was foolishly grateful out of her exasperation. "Yes, let's. Anything. I'll go mad if I sit around much longer. I'm not very well tuned to the country."

Missy closed herself out of the room too quietly. Griselda had been afraid to look at her eyes.

5

Danny and Ann were out of sight. Griselda pleated the window chintz between two fingers. When she turned into the room, David was gone. Missy was still plunged in the chair, her eyebrows pulled together. She began speaking tonelessly, obscenely, as if in a bad dream.

Griselda said, "I'm as bored as you are here. Why don't you get the twins to go back to New York?"

Missy laughed viciously. "They're yellow. All at once they're yellow. As if they could not take care of Con. I alone could take care of him. They are fools." She ground out the stub of one cigarette, lighted another immediately. David had warned Missy. She had promised but now she lighted another before the taste of the first was out of her mouth. They were not the depressive ones. Her eyes glistened; she could not sit quietly; her fingers moved, her throat. "Fools," she said. "They listen to no one. Not even me."

Griselda took a chair, not too near; a convenient chair, convenient for exit to the door if Missy should become—rabid. She suggested, "Maybe they've heard of Barjon Garth."

Missy leaned to her. "No one can do anything to the twins unless they allow it."

"That can't be true." She didn't want to antagonize the little fiend, but if she could only make her understand that the two weren't invincible, that even their evilness didn't make them not human, not invulnerable, maybe even now she could help Missy out of this hallucination. She said, "How do you think that, Missy? If they are cut shaving, don't they bleed? If they stumble, don't their ankles turn?" She didn't know what Missy's eyes said but she went on, almost harsh in her insistence. "What you mean is that usually they aren't hurt because they take the offensive. But if someone should strike first…"

Missy said rudely, "You talk too much. I'm going out."

"Alone?" Griselda repeated, "I'm bored too. Isn't there any way to get them started back to the city? They're waiting for Con, but he isn't coming. He's gone back to the border."

"How do you know? He was in Canaan this week."

"He had to go back. He has a job there." If she could but make

Missy believe. "He can't just sit around and do nothing. He isn't wealthy like the twins."

Missy laughed at her. "Maybe you think they're doing nothing." And then her eyes were narrow again. "I'm going out."

"For what?" Griselda stretched in the chair as if lazy, comfortable. "You know you can't endure walking and it's too cold to swim in the afternoon. Where's David?"

"He is probably asleep."

Griselda doubted it. He was probably in his plane, somewhere near he doubtless had one, or in that long dark car, going back to the city again, trying to coax Con to come into this trap. She was so weary of it all. She didn't care if Con did come. If he came, he'd know a way to get out of the nightmare. He was reckless and silly, but he was smart. She'd been wrong worrying about him. She'd forgotten how smart he was. She could weep for Con, to have Con holding her, protecting her from the horrors that were here.

Missy said cruelly, as if she could read her mind, "They're fools staying bottled up here while Con's probably taken the marble and beat it. They think Con will come here because you are here. He doesn't care that much for you. I don't think you're the type men care for. You're pretty enough but you're cold."

Griselda hated her. She wanted to say, "You think I'm cold because I can't stand your precious twins." But she didn't say it. She said something else, looking at Missy, not believing it. "You're my little sister."

Missy for the instant seemed real again, as if she'd come out of the web of drug she was weaving about herself. "That's right, I am." She spoke as strangely as Griselda had.

"We had the same father, a good father. The same mother— doesn't she care what happens to you, Missy?"

That bitter laugh came again. "She doesn't care what happens to any of us as long as we don't bother her in her toy palace." Again the laugh, more feline now. "It's a good thing she doesn't. We'd have to get rid of her too. As we did Marie Montefierrow when she got nosey."

Griselda exclaimed softly in horror, although she should have known before, "Oh, no!"

Missy's smile was evil. "Why not? You didn't believe that overdose of sleeping tablets, did you?"

And Griselda said again, sick, "Oh, no."

Missy licked her chops. "There's so many easy ways to get rid of people. After we get the marble..."

Griselda changed the subject wildly, foolishly, grasping for anything, "Why did they bring Ann here? Why drag her into this?" And knew her foolishness when Missy's eyes were slitted like a snake's.

"Because Danny wants beauty the way David wants power, the way you want clothes..."

The way Missy wants violence, hate, and the taste of blood. She couldn't let the ugly child go now. She kept her there talking, smoking, until her own throat was parched, and her body aching from the cramped chair. Until it was almost dusk, and Ann and Danny came noisily up on the porch, through the door. Ann was flushed from wind, her eyes bright, her hair blown. She was gay again, normal. Griselda stood quickly in her path, shielding her from Missy.

Danny threw down his stick across the chair. "O glorious walk!"

"It was. Glorious. And the sunset on the lake! Did you see it?"

"No." How to get Ann away quickly. There was a way. "You'd best go up and cream your face before it's roughed. I'll go with you." She clutched her sister's arm, almost ran her up to the bedroom. She heard Danny saying, "Get me a drink, Missy," and Missy's deliberately vicious, "Get your own god-damned drink, pig!"

She opened the door of the upper room, closed it quickly, put her back tight against it, to shut away what was to occur below. She cried out, "Ann, Ann, why did you go alone with Danny?"

Ann's fingertips were in the cream. "But it was perfectly all right, Griselda. He was charming, delightful. Really an interesting afternoon. He told me all about his set on the continent and it was amusing."

Griselda was defeated. She sagged against the door. There were only faint sounds from below. She had to try again. "Ann, it's dangerous. It's dangerous to stay here any longer. We've got to get away." She wouldn't let Ann be slaughtered as Nesta had been.

Ann answered, "No wonder you're morbid if you've been amusing Missy all afternoon. I do believe—" she wiped away the oiliness from her fingers—"I really do believe she's the cause of all the evil that you've mentioned. I don't believe the twins have one thing to do with it." The cream was laid on thickly, a mask on her face. She looked at her reflection. "I'll let it soak for ten minutes. I'll have time for that long a rest before dinner, I'm sure. And my feet are tired. We must have walked four miles."

Griselda touched the knob. "All right. Will you lock the door after me?"

Ann smiled. "Of course, dear, if you insist. But I do think you and I have been being geese."

Griselda waited until she heard the key turn in the lock. It was quiet below; she had been wrong; there wasn't a scene after all. She went down the stairs. Maybe there'd be a little peace; she could read something, get away momentarily from the horrible present. She turned into the living room, and then she shrank against the wall.

She had never seen hatred a living thing before, a twisted horrible living thing. But she saw Danny's eyes looking at Missy, she saw the curve of Missy's back, the projection of her head, one corner of her mouth. It was as if nothing could be more hideous, but it was, even as Griselda stood there, before she could leave as unnoticed as she came. Missy's fingers were a snake striking, there was the glint of steel from the stick there, and Danny's left cheek lay open, red, soft.

Griselda didn't scream. Her breath caught, her throat was swollen, her heart wasn't beating. The cane clanked as it fell. Missy's laughter shrieked as a madwoman's. "Danny…" She choked it in mirth, screaming it, "Oh, Danny!"

And then without warning she sprawled face down on the floor with yet another steel quivering in her back. David passed Griselda, standing there a part of the wall. She hadn't heard him come in, yet she had heard and not heard the porch door open, the footsteps. He pulled the steel out of Missy, walked to Danny, presented it to him. And then she did not scream, but groaned, sick to her marrow of death and violence and the slimy horror of these three. For Danny took the sword and without word or motion laid open David's cheek in a like thrust. They heard the groan. They turned their blank eyes and saw her there for the first time.

David said simply, "She tried to kill my brother."

6

She was rooted, she couldn't move even if she were the next to smear blood over the room. Nor did they move. And she wasn't frightened now for herself or for anyone. She was as dead as those they had killed.

She would be the next to lie motionless; she knew that now. Once they had the marble, they would do to her as they had to others, how many others no one would ever know. She could not be allowed to live; she knew them too well, had been with them too often when she should not have been. But it didn't matter. Not now. Nothing mattered except that they should have the marble and go away, go before they hurt others. Although it meant her death, although it meant that she could never again belong to Con, at least he should be safe, his gay recklessness preserved for someone else to love as she had loved him, and as he would never know.

She didn't want to look again but her eyes were there. Missy was so tiny, so young, flung down there on the floor. If you didn't see that soft crimson spreading, it was as if it were a child at rest. Missy needed to rest, she who had been restless all this day, so many days. Even as a child, she had never possessed peace. She had never belonged to a home and love and security as once had Griselda and Ann. She had been too young to know their father, his gentle pride of his daughters, his two, then three little daughters. It was Missy that their mother had taken away with her, not that she wanted her, not from her heart, but because she was too little to be left behind. No one had ever had time for Missy; no one had ever wanted her, no one until the twins came along.

It was better this way, better that she should be lying there, motionless forever. She couldn't have been taken away from them; she couldn't ever have understood. She wasn't a pathetic little figure sprawled down there; it was ridiculous to think of her that way. She was cruel and vicious; she'd been an unleashed evil, a dangerous animal, all the more dangerous because she was too young to want to understand. Yet somehow there was something about death that seemed to change all that, that made you fight tears stinging your nostrils, seeing her there, remembering incongruously a sleeping baby in a crib canopied in pale blue. Missy was alone again, lying there, lonely and unwanted as she'd been for those too many, too short, years. But now it needn't hurt; Missy didn't know; she would never know. She was gone.

Griselda turned her eyes away, back to the still motionless twins. She was glad Missy was dead, *glad!*

She said dully, "I'll give you the marble. Take me back and I'll give it to you." She didn't care what Con said, what Con thought. She didn't care if she was letting down all the X departments of the world. She couldn't let any more of this hideousness be unleashed.

She felt her way to the doorway, trying to choke back the nausea that pressed into her throat. She said, "Don't tell Ann what's happened." And, "I wish I'd given it to you a long time ago." Then she went blindly up to wake her sister.

XIV

THE CAR was at the door when they came flown. Griselda had made delay in the packing, but she was still afraid for Ann to pass the living room. She had to see before Ann did. It was clean. David and Danny were on the porch in the early dusk, their coats turned up about their cheeks, their hats pulled low over their eyes. The sticks were under their arms. Ann didn't notice. She didn't ask where the car had come from; she didn't care.

Danny climbed into the front. David helped Ann first, then Griselda, himself last, his left cheek by the window.

When the car started, Ann asked, "Isn't Missy coming?"

David's voice was without feeling. "No. She's staying here."

The drive in was silent. Everything was over, fatigued. Ann didn't understand, but the others knew it was the end. The twins weren't elated with their victory; they were gray as dream figures. Only when the glow of Riverside was against the sky did Griselda speak, in undertone to David.

"I'm going to take Ann up, get her settled. You can wait for me. You needn't be afraid I'll run away."

"I'm not."

Ann said, "I do wonder if Arthur's returned. I hope so. I feel like dancing tonight." So easily had she returned to East Seventy-ninth Street. She added, "Would you join us?"

David said, "No. We have business tonight."

Griselda said, "No." All she wanted was to get into a bed and sleep for a hundred years. To sleep, to wake and find this but a dream after all.

The car stopped at reality. Ann's apartment, tall and dark and strong. Ann said, "You needn't go up, Griselda."

"I want to." On the walk she spoke again to David. "I shan't be long." The clock in the lobby said that it wasn't yet ten o'clock.

It wasn't more than ten when she returned to the car.

David asked, "The apartment?"

She nodded. Might as well end it where it began. Might as well give Con one last chance to win. She could pretend once there that she must have at least until morning, make up some tale that it was impossible to get it for them before then. They didn't know but that it was in some vault somewhere. They didn't know the little blue stone was in her wadded handkerchief now, in her purse. She could hand it to them, never see them again—never see Con again! She knew they wouldn't let her live. But Con might be at the apartment, and faint chance that even now he might work it out. If she could speak to him, tell him of Missy, he would have the evidence that he and the X-men wanted. This time she had been there, eyewitness. Nor could the twins have had time to do away with all trace of the body. She knew that. Perhaps Con could win yet. He wasn't in danger, not now. She alone was. She held the marble and she would give it up. But not yet. Not until she took this final chance.

The car drew to the curb. David helped her out. Danny stood on the other side. It was like the first night but they weren't gay, laughing now. There were pain lines at their lips.

The elevator groaned to the first floor, clanked. They rode in that whimpering silence to the floor, and out.

Danny said, "There's someone inside—a light." Con was there. Impossible, yet he must be. She pushed the button keeping her finger tight on it. That would give Con a chance to prepare. She hid disappointment when Jasper Coldwater opened the door, abused, cross Jasper.

"Well, Griselda," he began.

She asked, "What are you doing here? I thought you were in California."

He sighed, "It's simply nauseous. More than I can bear, really. Inspector Tobin wouldn't let me go."

He walked away from the door and she and the twins followed. Then she saw Con. He was in pajamas, comfortable, lounging in a chair by the open window; of course, a glass in his hand. Seeing him, she knew she had been wrong. She shouldn't have brought the twins here, risked Con's safety in this way. Not that he seemed frightened; he didn't even look interested in anything but his drink. He greeted her casually, "So you came back home, baby. Tobin's been looking for you."

Danny's laugh was almost gay again. "Maybe this was supposed to be a trap. We don't trap easily."

"It wasn't…" But the buzz of the door broke her words. She was frozen. She hadn't heard the elevator. The twins had sticks sharply in their hands. She whispered, "What shall I do?" her eyes frightened.

David said, "I'll answer it."

"I'll hang my coat." Danny backed into the closet. There was the killer's smile on his lips.

She couldn't speak, she couldn't breathe, couldn't call out desperately, "Go away." She must let Tobin walk into this. And he and Con would try to keep the twins from getting away with the marble. She knew it. They wouldn't be afraid; they didn't know what the twins were really like.

David opened the door, shielding himself behind it. She stood watching the opening with sick, paralyzed eyes. And then she breathed. Only Gig.

David bowed. "Come in. We didn't expect you. We're about to have a drink. I'll fix them, Con."

Con waved his glass agreeably.

Gig looked different. She realized what it was. He was wearing his top coat and he didn't remove his hat. It was as if he were going away.

He asked David with little curiosity, "What happened to your face?"

"I believe I cut myself shaving." The smile flickered, went out. "Yes, that was it."

Jasper was testy. He turned on Danny. "I suppose you cut yourself, too."

He replied evenly, "I suppose I did."

David passed Griselda on his way to the kitchen cupboard. "Hadn't you better get what you came for? Then Danny and I can be on our way. After all, we weren't invited to this party."

Danny spoke. "We don't like to crash it, as you say."

"I'll get it," she said bluntly, but waited for Con to speak. But he said nothing. Maybe he hadn't heard.

"The *Normandie* sails at midnight, I believe. We can make it."

Jasper didn't understand any of this. "You can't sail without luggage and reservations."

Danny laughed at him soundlessly. "We can. We have."

Griselda went to the bedroom. She closed her eyes for an instant. She had been wrong, but she wasn't wrong now. She must ask for time. She mustn't give Con a chance to do anything about it. This must be done before Tobin came, before he and Con were together. Nothing would stop the twins now. Not if they had to kill everyone in the room. They should have the marble and go, go quietly, forever.

She took it from her bag, closed it into the hot palm of her hand and returned to the living room.

Con still lounged in the chair, still drinking. She looked at him, asking mute forgiveness for what she was about to do, what she must do. But he didn't understand. He only pantomimed the glasses on her nose as if he hadn't noticed before.

"So you were here Saturday."

She said, "Yes." He must have seen Irish before she had. Of course, Tobin with him. It didn't matter now. The police had her but she didn't care. After she gave the twins the blue marble they would go, the horror of them would be gone. She could endure whatever came after that.

David and Danny stood in the room between the others and the door. Their sticks were still under their arms carelessly, held by their elbows against their sides, but quicker than sound they could be touched. Gig was on the piano bench, his hands in his coat pockets.

She walked to David. "Here it is."

He held out his hand and she put the tiny ball, so round, so exquisitely blue, into his palm. He spoke with a certain exaltation, "The blue marble!" He touched it with one finger almost reverently and it fell apart. So it did open if you knew how. She could see the filigree etching of a map.

Gig's voice sounded. "You will have to take much care that the marble isn't stolen from you or that you aren't murdered by someone who wants it."

Everyone, save Jasper who was bored, looked at him, curious not at his words but that he should speak then. And he went on, "Need I say that if you move or attempt to touch your canes you will die, even as I am speaking. You know that. That is why you have not made the move. The same applies to all of you, even to Griselda." The revolver in his hand covered the room.

He spoke to the twins again, "If you will release your elbows—that is right." The sticks clattered to the floor. "Don't make any move with your feet. I know there is a gas pocket. You used it on me once, you recall. Griselda, please kick their sticks into the fireplace. No, don't pick them up, use your feet. Now, Griselda, if you will stand in front of the fireplace, your back to it. That is right."

She obeyed, feeling like Alice. It grew curiouser and curiouser. Gig now.

Gig said, "You, Mr. Coldwater, will extract Mr. Satterlee's artillery. Just keep your hands high, Mr. Satterlee, while he does it. Don't be afraid, Mr. Coldwater. I shan't hurt you, unless you should decide to try to use the guns. Just drop them at my feet."

David spoke. "You too have been after the marble?"

Gig smiled. "Yes. For many years. But if pleased me that you should acquire it for me, save me the—messy work—or much of it. Of course, I did have a few touches."

"Bette!" Griselda gasped.

"Yes," he admitted. "But nothing serious, Griselda. Only that she wouldn't recognize me. She interrupted my search here." He smiled again. "And now, Mr. Coldwater, you will take the marble from David and bring it to me." The gun did not waver as Jasper gingerly obeyed, plucking it from David's palm, hurrying across the room to lay it in Gig's. The tiny marble, but so very blue.

And again the buzzer sounded. Griselda's knees slumped. She held to the mantelpiece for support.

Con said, without moving, without concern, "It's probably Toby. Somebody better let him in or he may think something is wrong."

Jasper tittered.

Con said, "I mean we don't want him calling some dumb cops to bust in the door on us, do we? Edwin Booth, make yourself useful and open the door."

Jasper asked with some hauteur, "Are you speaking to me?"

"Yeah, you."

188 · DOROTHY B. HUGHES

Gig's gun was steady. He said, "Yes, Mr. Coldwater, you had best open it."

Jasper sighed. His face showed that he wasn't used to being ordered around like one of his own servants. But he didn't like that pointed gun. He scurried like a rabbit, let Tobin in.

Gig stated, "Mr. Coldwater will take your gun, Inspector Tobin."

"Never carry one." Tobin walked on into the room as if none of this were happening. "Looks like I'm a little late, Con."

"Looks like it," Con replied. "Moore with you?"

"He came up the back way."

Griselda turned her head. Moore was there, lounging in the bedroom doorway. She heard him say, "Look quick, Toby! Give Griselda a hand."

She had known she couldn't stand there much longer. She was beginning to weave like a buoy. Tobin caught her, dropped her without ado into a chair. Danny asked, "Shall I get whiskey?"

Gig answered, "Stay where you are. I still have the gun pointed, you see."

Con drawled, "You might as well put it down, Zcrsky. I filled it up with blanks today while you were down seeing about a passport."

Gig looked first puzzled, then incredulous.

Con lit a cigarette. "My God, didn't you know we've had a tail on you for weeks?"

Tobin put in his word. "And if any of the rest of you have any bright ideas about retrieving your artillery, just skip it. Moore's got more medals than anybody on the force for target practice. Quick on the draw, too, aren't you, Cowboy?"

Moore looked embarrassed, thumbs in his belt, but he nodded.

Tobin said, "There's some X-men downstairs. Garth's on his way now from Washington. And is he tickled to have you twins safe at last."

David bowed slightly. "Why does he want us? We've done nothing."

"He might ask a few questions about how you happened to get hold of the blue marble."

David smiled. "We don't have the blue marble, Inspector. Herr Gigland—or is it Zcrsky?—has it."

Con said, "Zcrsky's the name, and by the way, Zcrsk, I found where you'd hidden Gig. That's one reason I've been so tied up, babe." This was to Griselda.

Tobin said, "Marble or no marble, twins, you'll get yours. The X is handling and they've finally got enough against you to put you both away for good."

Con added, "We've even got your pilot that forced my plane down and took Irish away so you could kill him."

The twins did not speak. Gig did. He laid the emasculated gun carefully on the piano bench. "You will let me go, please. I have done nothing wrong. I am not a killer, as these."

Con said, "Garth's been looking for you too, you know, Zcrsky." He unfolded himself from the chair and started across to him. "You might as well hand back the marble. It won't do you any good now."

Gig's calm was frenzy immediately. He backed nearer the window. He shrilled, "I won't give you the marble! I won't! I've waited too long for it! It's mine!" Con took another step towards him and Gig screamed in his fury, "Don't touch me! This is mine, mine!" He wasn't normal; he knew he was cornered. He thrust his hand behind him out of Con's reach, but he had forgotten the open window. He stumbled against it, grasped at the ledge to keep from falling—and the marble slipped from his palm. He whirled, clawing for it, but it rolled away, over the edge, down, down, four stories to the street below. There was no sound in the room but Gig's sobbing, Danny's quick intake of breath.

David drew back. "It will not be found. It will be a thousand years before it comes to light again." His black eyes, unseeing eyes, turned again to the room. "It has all been a waste." He buttoned his coat, adjusted his scarf, his hat. He took one of the gold mono-grammed cigarettes from his case, lighted it with deliberation. Every eye watched him, watched the match burn evenly, his in-take of smoke, the trickle that came from his mouth. Every eye watched Danny follow the same motions, as if synchronized with his brother.

Danny repeated, "It has all been a waste."

They turned together, moved steadily to the door. David said, "Goodnight, Griselda," and Danny smiled, "It's been fun seeing you." It was the same as it had been too many times before, save that now there were no sticks beneath their arms. They opened the door, went out, closing it behind them.

Griselda was laughing and crying, her arms about Jasper of all that room; Jasper, because he alone was undisturbed, only terribly annoyed. He was not playing the lead tonight

Tobin said, "They can't get away. The X are waiting for them below."

Griselda whispered, but everyone heard her. "They won't be taken. They can do things no human people can do." She be-lieved it.

Con shook himself, wiped his forehead. "For God's sake, let's have a drink."

2

As if a fog lifted, the confusion went away. Uniforms came for Gig, departed. Jasper made relieved and determined exit. Only Tobin, Moore, Con and she remained, glasses in hand. She sat close to

Con on the couch, so close she could feel the warmth of his arm under his coat sleeve.

Con said, "Sure glad you and Moore got back in time, Toby. I couldn't have done anything to stop anybody."

Tobin told Griselda, "We just missed you."

"Missed me?"

"Con sent us up to Queechy to bring you back. He was getting nervous. We flew up, but you'd already gone. The place was empty, so we flew back in double time."

She caught her lip in her teeth. "Empty. Missy—"

Con touched her hand.

"There wasn't anyone there."

She closed her eyes again, trying to forget that scarlet room. Maybe another spring Missy would be helping the violets and wild roses and little ferns to grow. Maybe she'd be under the water forever. The twins knew ways.

Tobin said, "It would have been just too bad, wouldn't it, if Zcrsky had examined his artillery before dropping in tonight?"

Con shook his head. "He'd have had to go out for more shells. And the tail would have let me know. I cleaned him out today with Bette watching and she fidgety as a bird."

Griselda wondered, "Why didn't Bette tell me Gig wasn't the real Gig?"

Con said, "I asked her that. She didn't know you thought he was my Gig. To her any Gigland was rightly called Gig, and he told her the same yarn he told the University about J. Antwerp going off to Persia. He even forged a letter to her—of course, Gig's letter to Columbia was forgery—warning her about saying anything of J. Antwerp being away, that he was on a very secret mission. He actually needn't have gone to that trouble. Bette never has been much of a talker." He put out his cigarette. "He was no more a Gigland than you are, of course."

Griselda shook her head. "What happens to him? He was good to me."

"If he hadn't made the mistake of kidnaping Gig and shutting him up in a hole of a tenement, he'd only be kicked out of the country. But kidnaping's serious business. Thank God," he drank, "Gig's all right. Anyhow he will be when he gets a shave and bath and some sleep." He drained his glass. "I'm going to have a refill."

Griselda said she'd have another. He'd have to come back beside her to bring it. If she missed the plane, Jasper would go on anyway. If Tobin and Moore would only leave, maybe Con would realize her. Maybe he'd think her too weak to be setting out this night for California, not know that she was only trembling at his nearness.

She didn't want to go back to California. She didn't ever want to go away from him again. But what else could she do when Con was silent, letting Jasper make plans. He had said, "Let's leave on the next plane, Griselda, get out of this revolting town and go home to Hollywood."

She had tried to hesitate, give Con a chance to demur, but he had said nothing. He hadn't even looked at her while Jasper went on spoiling things as carefully as Aunt Charlotte or Ann might spoil them. "You might just as well, you know. My picture goes into production right away and Oppy wants you to design the women's clothes. He's expecting you. There's really no sense of your staying in New York any longer. And the trip is so nauseating alone. I'll go pack and pick you up, shall I?"

Con silent. You couldn't stay on when you weren't asked. She had said, not looking at either of them, I'll meet you at the airport."

Con might have thought she wanted to go. Even now as close to him as she dared move herself, he might not know. If she were alone with him… But she couldn't ask the others to get out.

She said, "Thank you," when Con returned, taking the fresh glass. His hand just brushed hers. Her fingers ached to retain the touch.

He began talking again, keeping Tobin and Moore there, "We could have cleaned this up last week, only I had to find Gig. I was afraid of what might have happened to him. Garth helped. He's been trying to land Zcrsky for a long time. Get him out of the country. He may have been good to you, but he's wanted under more than one name in more than one place."

Her fingers just touched his sleeve. "Con, why did you risk keeping the marble here in the apartment?"

He knew her touch was there. "It wasn't the real one, baby. It looked like it but it was only a late Renaissance imitation." Then he guffawed to Toby, "Where do you think she hid it? Sewed inside a kid's rag doll!"

Her eyes opened wide to his. "You opened my deposit box? You read that letter!"

"Sure," he said. "Who do you think I am, Sir Galahad?"

There was silence between them for that swift, startled moment. He must have felt her tremble, the glass in her hand was as in wind. She couldn't believe. She didn't dare believe. But his look was as it had been long ago, as if he too wished they were alone to clear up so many things. Her eyes dropped. She could explain later that she was sentimental the night she wrote it and frightened, terribly frightened for him.

Tobin glancing from Con to her suddenly seemed aware. "We'd better hump, Moore. Trouble is soon as one case is out of the way, a new one starts. Morning comes early."

The sergeant downed his drink. "Sure does."

Tobin stood up and stretched. "Give you a lift, Griselda?"

She held her breath for one momentous instant.

Con answered. "No, she's staying here."

She didn't look at him.

He was walking to the door with the men. He was saying, "She came East for a rest and now she's going to have it. We're going to spend a week in bed."

AMERICAN MYSTERY CLASSICS
from PENZLER PUBLISHERS

Established by Otto Penzler in early 2018, the American Mystery Classics series is a line of newly-reissued mystery and detective fiction from the years between the first and second World Wars, also known as the genre's Golden Age.

Our carefully-curated titles include celebrated classics by authors including Erle Stanley Gardner, Ellery Queen, and Mary Roberts Rinehart, each one refreshed with attractive new covers and contextualized with original introductions.

With more than forty years of experience as an editor, critic, publisher, and bookseller, Otto Penzler's selections are made with unparalleled expertise, meaning that the series is sure to please both long-time fans as well as newcomers to the genre.

Visit penzlerpublishers.com to see more upcoming authors and titles.

Available Now:

Ellery Queen
The Chinese Orange Mystery
An Ellery Queen Mystery

"Without doubt the best of the Queen stories."
—*The New York Times Book Review*

Introduction by Otto Penzler

The offices of foreign literature publisher and renowned stamp collector Donald Kirk are often host to strange activities, but the most recent occurrence—the murder of an unknown caller, found dead in an empty waiting room—is unlike any that has come before. Nobody, it seems, entered or exited the room, and yet the crime scene clearly has been manipulated, leaving everything in the room turned backwards and upside down. Stuck through the back of the corpse's shirt are two long spears and a tangerine is missing from the fruit bowl. Enter amateur sleuth Ellery Queen, who arrives just in time to witness the discovery of the body, only to be immediately drawn into a complex case in which no clue is too minor or too glaring to warrant careful consideration.

Reprinted for the first time in over thirty years, *The Chinese Orange Mystery* is revered to this day for its challenging conceit and inventive solution. The book is a "fair play" mystery in which readers have all the clues needed to solve the crime. In 1981, the novel was selected as one of the top ten locked room mysteries of all time by a panel of mystery-world luminaries that included Julian Symons, Edward D. Hoch, Howard Haycraft, and Otto Penzler.

PB ISBN 978-1-61316-106-7, $15.95 • HC ISBN 978-1-61316-110-4, $25.95

Available Now:

Mary Roberts Rinehart
The Red Lamp

"There are a few masters in the field of crime who never stale, and Mary Roberts Rinehart is one of the select group." —*Kirkus*

Introduction by Otto Penzler

An all-around skeptic when it comes to the supernatural, literature professor William Porter gives no credence to claims that Twin Towers, the seaside manor he's just inherited, might be haunted. So, though his wife, more attuned to spiritual disturbance, refuses to occupy the main house, Porter convinces her to spend a summer in the lodge elsewhere on the grounds. But not long after they arrive, Porter sees the evidence of haunting that the townspeople speak of: a shadowy figure illuminated by the red light of Horace's writing lamp, the very light that shone on the scene of his death. And though he isn't convinced that it is a spirit and not a man, Porter knows that, whichever it is, the figure is responsible for the rash of murders—first of sheep, then of people—that breaks out across the countryside. When the suspect eludes his pursuit, Porter risks implicating himself in the very crimes he hopes to solve.

Written with atmospheric prose and tension that rises with every page, *The Red Lamp* is a hybrid of murder mystery and gothic romance that shows the "American Agatha Christie" at the height of her powers.

PB ISBN 978-1-61316-102-9, $15.95 • HC ISBN 978-1-61316-113-5, $25.95

Available Now:

Clayton Rawson
Death From a Top Hat
A Great Merlini Mystery

"A cornerstone of detective fiction."
—*The New York Times*

Introduction by Otto Penzler

Now retired from the tour circuit on which he made his name, master magician The Great Merlini spends his days running a magic shop in New York's Times Square and his nights moonlighting as a consultant for the NYPD. The cops call him when faced with crimes so impossible that they can only be comprehended by a magician's mind. In the most recent case, two occultists are discovered dead in locked rooms, one spread out on a pentagram, both appearing to have been murdered under similar circumstances. The list of suspects includes an escape artist, a professional medium, and a ventriloquist, so it's clear that the crimes took place in a realm that Merlini knows well. But in the end it will take his logical skills, and not his magical ones, to apprehend the killer.

Reprinted for the first time in over twenty years, *Death From a Top Hat* is an ingeniously-plotted puzzle set in the world of New York stage magic, which was at its pinnacle in the early twentieth century. In 1981, the novel was selected as one of the top ten locked room mysteries of all time by a panel of mystery-world luminaries that included Julian Symons, Edward D. Hoch, Ellery Queen's co-creator Frederic Dannay, and Otto Penzler.

PB ISBN 978-1-61316-106-7, $15.95 • HC ISBN 978-1-61316-110-4, $25.95

Available Now:

Craig Rice
Home Sweet Homicide

"The doyenne of the comic mystery"
—*Kirkus*

Introduction by Otto Penzler

Unoccupied and unsupervised while mother is working, the children of widowed crime writer Marion Carstairs find diversion wherever they can. So when the kids hear gunshots at the house next door, they jump at the chance to launch their own amateur investigation—and after all, why shouldn't they? They know everything the cops do about crime scenes, having read about them in mother's novels. They know what her literary detectives would do in such a situation, how they would interpret the clues and handle witnesses. Plus, if the children solve the puzzle before the cops, it will do wonders for the sales of mother's novels. But this crime scene isn't a game at all; the murder is real, and when its details prove more twisted than anything in mother's fiction, they'll have to enlist Marion's help to sort them out. Or is that just part of their plan to hook her up with the lead detective on the case?

The basis for the 1946 film with the same name, *Home Sweet Homicide* is the novel that launched Craig Rice to literary fame. The book, a comedic crime story that pokes fun at the conventions of the genre, finds "the Dorothy Parker of detective fiction" at her most entertaining.

PB ISBN 978-1-61316-103-6, $15.95 • HC ISBN 978-1-61316-112-8, $25.95

Available Now:

Stuart Palmer
The Puzzle of the Happy Hooligan
A Hildegarde Withers Mystery

"*The Puzzle of the Happy Hooligan* is a book that will keep you laughing and guessing from the first page to the last." — *The New York Times*

Introduction by Otto Penzler

Hildegarde Withers is just your average school teacher—with above-average skills in the art of deduction. The New Yorker often finds herself investigating crimes led only by her own meddlesome curiosity, though her friends on the NYPD don't mind when she solves their cases for them. After plans for a grand tour of Europe are interrupted by Germany's invasion of Poland, Miss Withers heads to sunny Los Angeles instead, where her vacation finds her working as a technical advisor on the set of a film adaptation of the Lizzie Borden story. The producer has plans for an epic retelling of the historical killer's patricidal spree—plans which are derailed when a screenwriter turns up dead. While the local authorities quickly deem his death accidental, Withers suspects otherwise and calls up a detective back home for advice. The two soon team up to catch a wily killer.

At once a pleasantly complex locked room mystery and a hilarious look at the foibles of Hollywood, *The Puzzle of the Happy Hooligan* finds Palmer, a screenwriter himself, at his most perceptive. Reprinted for the first time in over thirty years, this riotously funny novel shows why Hildegarde Withers was among the most beloved detectives of Golden Age American mystery novel.

PB ISBN 978-1-61316-106-7, $15.95 • HC ISBN 978-1-61316-110-4, $25.95